Found by You

A. Boss

PEAK EVEREST PUBLISHING

When he takes the trash out without having to be asked.

"It's the little things."

Prologue.

Maci

The funeral procession comes to a halt along the gravel drive at the center of the cemetery, and my gut roils.

I tried to prepare myself, knowing I'd see Evan's wife—or widow, I should say—but being here now…it's overwhelming. My head still swims at the realization for the hundredth time in the last week.

My life has been turned upside down and I'm now standing on the outskirts of the catalyst that ruined it all. None of this would have happened if I had known Evan was a married man. I would've never *ever* started a relationship with him, and in turn, there's a good chance he'd still be alive today.

You can't carry that on your conscience, Maci, it wasn't your fault.

It doesn't feel that way.

I can't help wondering if I hadn't told him, maybe then he wouldn't have been driving so recklessly, maybe then he wouldn't have had a blood alcohol level of 0.2—maybe *then* he wouldn't have been black-out drunk and speeding down the freeway.

The only upside for my weighted conscience is he didn't hurt anyone else besides himself.

He hurt you...

I give my head a light shake to clear the thought. Evan hurt a lot of people, not just me. I mean, he ruined my reputation, my family refuses to speak to me, the people I once called my 'friends' continue to ignore my calls, I lost my job—one might say, he ruined my life.

All because I fell for a pretty boy in a pretty uniform, who promised me forever when he was already taken.

I sigh, watching silently as six, fully-dressed military men act as the formal pall-bearers of Evan's coffin. Family members solemnly follow the casket to the assigned plot in the fifth row where the funeral is set to take place any moment now.

My hand rests over my low belly, shielding it. I'm not welcome here, I know. But it didn't feel right to *not* come. So here I'll stand, far enough away that I won't cause a scene while paying my respects to the man I thought I loved, but who never loved me.

"You shouldn't be here." The words are a harsh, feminine hiss filled with hate and anger and grief. My heart aches at the emotional wave as I face Evan's widow. I was so lost in the moment, I didn't hear her approach.

She's beautiful even in the throes of her loss. Tall and blonde with exceptional features. I'd only seen pictures of her in the paper—their wedding photos, nonetheless.

"I'm sorry I—" The echo of her slap registers before the sting across my cheek.

"Leave," she shouts with venom as a man comes up behind her, gently escorting her away from me with hushed words.

I suck in a sharp breath. Tears pool in my eyes as an older man lingers nearby, likely making sure I heed the widow's warning and go, but not yet.

I stare out at the vast green of the cemetery, forcing myself to take it all in. The greying sky, the solemn crowd continuing to grow in attendance for the fallen war hero, and the hateful glares in my direction as Evan's widow reunites with her family across the way—I accept it all.

You didn't know. And they don't care.

I'm the dirty mistress in their eyes. The one who seduced their beloved husband, son, friend—then killed him with my existence.

With *our* existence.

My hand falls back to my side. There's no use in dwelling over it any longer. What's done is done, as they say. I tug my coat tighter around me as I head to the parking lot. The older man gives me a stiff nod when I pass, as if he approves of my retreat.

Guilt nearly chokes me once I reach my car and get inside. The realization that no one wants me—not here, not anywhere—hits me all at once with a wracking sob.

I'm just the *whore* who had an affair with the governor's son-in-law—his daughter's husband. I'm no longer welcome here. The entire state of Oklahoma has made that glaringly apparent.

Leave, she said.

And I intend to.

One.

Duke

"WE'RE HAVING A BABY," Cassidy, my brother Butch's fiancée, announces over dinner at my parents.

My chest tightens.

My mother, Julie, leaps from her seat to hug Cassidy, then Butch. "Oh, my baby is having a baby," she coos, tears in her eyes.

Butch and Cassidy have been living together for nearly four months. It was a mere month ago when my brother finally mustered up the courage and asked Cassidy to marry him.

If I thought the idea of attending my brother's wedding hurt... It doesn't compare to this.

I should be happy for them. I *need* to be happy for them, but it's so fucking hard when I had it all and lost it in a blink of an eye that was in the shape of a plane crash.

Five years ago, that same blink took the love of my life, my high school sweetheart, my wife, Rachel...along with our unborn child.

She was only six weeks at the time. We hadn't even announced it to our families yet. Rachel wanted to wait until the first doctor's appointment before we made any kind of announcement. She was on her way to visit her sister in Billings, eager for her to be the first to know.

Then the plane went down—engine failure, they told me—taking the lives of all four on board.

It took five, if you ask me.

Being a father was a silent dream of mine. Silent to those around me, but not to her. Rachel and I knew we wanted kids. *A crap ton.* Her words, not mine. And I was all for it. Kids weren't a hard sell. I wanted them just as bad, if not more.

Now...five years later, she's gone, and I'm still fumbling to pick up the pieces of what I thought was my future.

I've bought the neighboring property between my brothers, Butch and Beau, right up the road from our folks' place. I even started building my dream home with the help of our other brothers, Rhett and Levi, a few months ago.

Moving on with my life these last few years has been hard in itself. Planning for the future has brought a whole different kind of hurt I didn't anticipate when I started this endeavor four months ago with putting my house up for sale.

I'm renting out one of Beau's vacation rental cabins on his mountainside property. He's got two built at the moment, and since being stationed overseas for the last eighteen months, my parents and siblings help with maintenance and booking them on his behalf.

There are five of us Montgomery sons. All of us own and operate our own businesses. If there's one thing people know from the last name Montgomery, it's that we don't do anything half-assed—I sure as hell didn't.

Montgomery Repair & Towing. I eat, breathe, and sleep my business. Trucks, cars, the occasional motorcycle and boat—I *live* for the classic shit. Old, new, and everywhere in between. We're the #1 go-to repair shop in all of Whitetail, Montana, and the three surrounding counties. I've built a solid standard with my reputation.

Butch and I are close, being a year apart and looking like damn twins, we were raised as such. Beau's always been the loner of the siblings, straight laced with a stick up his ass eighty percent of the time. Leaving Rhett and Levi close enough to start their company together.

But when it comes to the big events, we always make it about the group. And with a wedding and a baby on the way...the Montgomerys are only growing.

"Congratulations," my father, Clayton, chimes in, hugging the soon-to-be parents.

Butch gives me a concerned glare at my silence, and I take the cue, doing my damnedest to keep my voice even despite the unwanted emotions building inside of me. "Congratulations, guys."

Rhett and Levi give their cheers, and as the conversation shifts to talk about the baby and due date—all I hear is *six weeks*, and I cringe.

I physically cringe because I can't help myself. The memories are subtle, fading by the day, but that feeling I had when Rachel told me she was pregnant...

That's a feeling I'll never forget.

"So, what you're saying is, the night Butch proposed...he gave you a little...early wedding gift?" Lily laughs.

Cassidy nods, beaming a smile with happy tears in her eyes. "I guess so."

Butch scoffs, wrapping his arm around Cassidy and pulling her into his side. When he kisses her on the temple, I decide it's time to go.

"Well, thanks for dinner, Ma," I say, standing from my seat, "but I've got some late snow plowing to get done if I plan to open shop on time tomorrow."

My mother gives me a hard look, and I already know I'll hear shit about this from her on the phone at some point. Going around the table, I say my goodbyes. When I reach Cassidy, I give her a long hug as she whispers, "Are you okay?"

I clear my throat as I step away from her. "Congrats again, guys. Can't wait for the little shit kicker to get here."

She smiles weakly when Butch lifts his chin, standing. "I'll walk you out."

I head to the front door of my parents' old farmhouse. It's gone through a few renovations over the years with the help of my siblings, but it still holds its rustic country charm. A family home, through and through.

One I hope to emulate someday.

Yanking on my steel-toed boots and Carhartt jacket, I walk outside with Butch hot on my heels. *And he thinks* I'm *the annoying one.*

"We were going to tell you first," he says. "But, uh, you've been so busy lately. No one's seen you around."

"Don't worry about it," I say, reaching my blacked-out company-wrapped truck with *Montgomery Repair & Towing* written in a bold silver and harsh red with a steel plow on the front. "I'm happy for you guys. You deserve this, Butch."

He pushes his hands in his pockets, eyeing me as I hop in the driver's seat. "So do you, ya know," he huffs, forcing a cloud of steam from his nostrils and into the cold, mid-December night. "That's what you told me, isn't it? If even a prick like me can find it, you can find it again."

My jaw tightens, my resolve crumbling to mere ash. "And what if I don't want to find it again, Butch, huh? No woman I've met for the last five years has changed a goddamn thing for me. I'm done looking, all right? I'll do ya one better. I'll be the brother who dies alone on this fuckin' mountain. How's that sound? 'Cause it sounds damn good to me," I bite out, slamming the door as I start my truck.

Butch goes to grab the door, but I lock it. He bangs on the window, trying to tell me something about *not leaving like this*. I ignore him and peel out down the snowy driveway.

The last person I'll be taking any kind of relationship advice from is one of my damn brothers.

Two.

Maci

"Life is a highway..." I whisper-sing to myself as I get back in my white Chevy Equinox after filling the gas tank.

I'm back on the snow-dusted roads a moment later in what I *think* is either Wyoming or Montana, but I'm not sure anymore. My GPS has been cutting in and out for the last hour as I make my way through the mountains. I should stop for the night, but I've got a schedule to keep. And I need to go as far as I can so when I pay for a motel room, I can keep it for a whole day to rest—not just half a night with their annoying early checkouts.

I crank up the heat and place a hand over my belly, sighing to myself at the rumble that follows. "Just a little bit longer, sweet pea, then we'll find a room and somewhere to eat, I promise."

Talking to my belly at only ten weeks pregnant might seem a little weird to most, but when you're driving alone from Oklahoma to Alaska, you take what conversation you can get. Even if it is a growing fetus in your womb.

Most people would say I'm crazy for running away how I am. That things will 'die down' in time—they won't. And even if they do, what's the point? There's nothing left for me in Oklahoma. Not after...everything.

He ruined my life. *Years* of my life wasted on someone who was a walking, talking, good-looking lie. And I hate myself for getting so wrapped around his finger the way I did.

Evan Dunn. The worst mistake of my life, and the father to my unborn child. *My* child. It all came crashing down when I found out I was pregnant. While I was excited at the prospect of starting a family with him, Evan demanded we get rid of it. When I told him I wanted to keep the baby... He lost it.

Secrets were revealed. Lines were crossed.

My world went up in flames the next morning when his face was plastered on every news outlet: The Governor's son-in-law *dead* from a fatal car accident...

Pictures faded in and out on the screen, from his military photo to the one of him and his wife on their wedding day.

I feel just as sick now as I did then.

I was the other woman.

The woman no one wants to be. Not really, anyway. And I had no idea. He should have been an actor for the deceit he was able to pull over my eyes. But no one cares about my side of the story. No one wants to hear that *I didn't know*—no matter how true the statement may be.

When the story made the news and the investigation into foul play began shortly after...my name was written alongside the scandal to rock the state.

While the police and detectives believed my story—and all the proof I had to back it up—it was too late. Words were spun to paint me as the villain in every aspect of the term. I had hoped my family and friends would realize the truth. I mean, they're the ones who should know me best, right?

Wrong.

"There's no way you couldn't have known he was married."

"Do you get off on being a homewrecker?"

"Who hired you? Was this some sort of political stunt you're pulling?"

The statements and accusations were so far from the truth, I wonder if they ever knew me at all.

I may only be twenty-six going forward with this whole *single mom thing*, but I've never been more sure of something in my life.

So, yeah, between the pure embarrassment, being ostracized from my family, and the dirty looks from everyone I've ever known—it was time to go.

Alaska is the final destination, and I've probably picked a crappy time to be driving across half-a-dozen states, a large chunk of Canada, and the mass of Alaska to get to Anchorage.

At least I'll be in a snowy wonderland for Christmas. It's the little things.

My car does a funky jolt, snapping me out of my thoughts as I start to lose speed. Pressing harder on the gas, the speedometer continues to go down. I've got the pedal to the floor, but nothing's happening. *Shit.* I push the button for my hazard lights and ease onto the side of the road.

Throwing it in park, I kill the engine and try the only thing I can think of... I wait a few beats, then go to start it again. *Click, click, click.*

"No, no, no," I whimper at the dreaded death click. I desperately try to pump my brake, hoping for a miracle, but...no such luck.

Story of my life.

I lift my gaze to the windshield to gauge where I am. Of course, there isn't a street light, sign, mile marker, not even a car or house in sight. And it doesn't help it's freaking pitch black out. *Are there even lines on this road?*

I grab my phone, noting it's just after nine, and attempt to refresh my GPS that's been 'searching' since I stopped at the gas station over an hour ago. I wait, hopeful the single bar of service doesn't—

No service glares back at me.

I'm officially dead in the water with no clue as to where I am.

"Shit." With shaky hands, I grab my coat, pull it on, and get out. Shivering, I hold my phone up, trying for a signal to—at the very least—get my GPS back on track. I'll need a location to give someone when I call for help. I pace the desolate street, taking minor steps left and right, my phone held high over my head.

Nothing.

Not a single blip of service.

Like an unwitting victim in a horror movie, I spin around in a panic as the wind picks up, causing a rattle in the trees. My stomach twists, and a wave of nausea hits me like a freight train.

I tug my coat tighter around me and take a deep breath, reaching in and popping the hood. "We're okay, we're okay," I whisper, continuing to look around as I walk to the front of my car.

Not that I know a single thing about cars, but it doesn't hurt to check, right? Who knows, I might get lucky for once in my life and it's a silly stick I ran over or something. I push the hood up and stare at the engine expecting—what, I'm not sure.

Hot tears sting my eyes. This can't be happening.

Breathe, Maci, breathe. Figure this out.

After taking in a few calming breaths with full-blown tears streaming down my face, I step around the car to get inside and warm up a bit when a set of headlights appear in the distance.

And they're coming this way.

"Oh, thank god," I breathe.

With my hazards blinking and my headlights still on, I stand beside the hood of my car and cross my fingers whoever this is will see me and stop. However, they don't seem to be slowing.

I start waving my arms wildly, yelling out, "Stop, please!"

The truck finally starts to slow, nearly blowing right past me. It's big, I note, black with a logo I can't read written along the sides and a large yellow plow on the front. Thankfully, they pull off to the side in front of my car and begin backing up.

I stand by the hood of my car, shifting nervously from foot to foot before stuffing my hand in my coat pocket. My hand wraps around the small, chilled can of pepper spray I've kept on my person for the last three weeks. I've never had to use it, thankfully, but when I started receiving threats on my life from random governor supporters, it seemed like a safe bet. And I *really* don't want to use it on this person, but being stranded in the middle of—who knows where—pregnant and alone... I'll spray The Pope if he's a threat.

Full on Mama Bear.

The driver of the truck turns on their hazard lights before parking, and the first thing out the driver's door is a huge black boot. I swallow hard as a broad, tower of a man steps out.

My palm goes clammy as I tighten my hold on the pepper spray that doesn't seem like enough to put this man down if I need to. Can I even reach his face? He has to be over a foot taller than me, and at my short five-foot-two, I'm not even sure if the stream of toxic spray would phase him.

I take him in as he approaches. He's got a black baseball cap pulled low over his eyes, a strong jaw locked tight with a few days' worth of chestnut scruff growing on it. Wearing a pair of dark wash jeans, a black hoodie, and a brown Carhartt jacket—all of which do *nothing* to hide the clear brute strength this man possesses.

He's tall, broad, clearly strong, and I'm feeling smaller by the second as he comes to stand before me. *Gulp.*

"Are you hurt, ma'am?" His voice is a deep, *deep* baritone growl that sends shivers up and down my spine.

"N-No," I force out, gesturing to the opened hood. "It's my car. I don't know what happened. I just lost all power, and I don't seem to have any cell service. Do you have a phone I could use by chance?"

"This section of the road is a dead zone," he tells me, shifting his attention to under the hood of my car. He reaches in, messing with...who the heck knows. "Get in and try to start it."

"O-oh, okay," I say, unsure before hurrying into the front seat and attempting to start it like he told me to. The car turns over some, and just when I think it might fire up...it goes dead.

"Stop," he shouts, and I do. He slams the hood closed, and my stomach drops.

Is...that it? Did he fix it?

I get out, holding the door as if my life depends on it. *Let this one thing go right, please.*

"Your transmission is blown and you've got oil pouring out the pan. You're not going anywhere in this," he says sternly, my heart sinking lower with every word. "Town is about ten miles north. Phone service kicks back up in another mile or two. I can give you a ride, call a tow, get this taken wherever you want."

I shiver, and hug into myself, not able in the slightest to stop the tears from flowing. I'm not sure how much more I can take of this—this thing where nothing can go right and everything goes wrong. "Where, um, should I send it?"

He's silent for a moment. "You're not from around here, are you?"

Is it that obvious?

I shake my head. If the admission gets me chopped into tiny pieces with him wearing my skin as a suit, then so be it. It'd be the cherry on top at this point.

The man sighs heavily, scratching his chin and gesturing over his shoulder. "I own a repair shop in town. I'll call one of my guys to come out and tow your car in for the night," he says, giving his chin a jerk toward my car. "Grab what you need and leave the keys on the front seat."

My eyes widen. "I-I can't do that. Everything I own is in this car," I blurt out, then promptly cringe at how that makes me sound homeless—even though I *sort of* am. I mean, I have a portable storage unit waiting for my call to deliver, but the majority of my belongings that are important to me...yeah, they're stuffed in the back at the moment.

"You're living in this car?"

"No, I'm, uh, moving."

"Moving," he repeats as he leans down, peering in my car. "Where you movin' to?"

My eyes narrow, suspicion seeping in. "That's none of your business, *buddy*. Now, if you'll just—"

"Duke," he grumbles. "My name's Duke Montgomery, I own Montgomery Repair & Towing."

Of course, he does. "Well, *Duke*, I can't leave my car here with all my belongings for just anyone to come by and take." Do people around here really leave their cars unlocked like he's telling me to do now? Surely not.

Duke huffs. "All right, fine, how much shit you got?"

"Excuse me?"

"How much *stuff* do you have?" he asks again, a bit more condescending than before. "I've got room in the backseat; I'll take you to wherever it is you're goin'."

"I'm..." I trail off, not able to stop the tears. I turn away, wiping roughly at my cheeks as I start to cry. *Dammit, Maci, you should've stopped at that last rest stop.*

How do I tell this guy that—I *don't* know—I have nowhere to go besides a cheap motel?

"I didn't mean to upset you, ma'am," he says, and I can't tell if he's annoyed or sorry. "If you'd like to get your purse at least, we can ride up the road for service. I'll make a call and get the tow out here while we wait."

A harsh gust of freezing wind whips across my face and my tears turn to ice over my cheeks.

"I'm going to need a decision here, ma'am. There's a storm coming in, and I'd rather not be out here when it hits."

Of course, there's a storm coming—because why wouldn't there be? My luck never ceases to amaze me. And what choice do I have?

I nod quickly, leaning in my car to grab my purse and phone charger. Duke holds the door to keep the wind from closing it on me as I get what I need. Reaching in the backseat, I take my pre-packed duffle containing basic toiletries, a few changes of clothes, and my laptop.

Duke takes the duffle from me. "Turn off the headlights and leave the hazards on," he instructs. "Keys on the front seat."

I do as he says, even if I hesitate for a second before dropping my keys into an unlocked vehicle, then follow his lead to his truck. I squint, trying to focus enough to read the company-wrapped name now that he isn't speeding past me. *Montgomery Repair & Towing*. At least he was telling the truth about that. There's a phone number alongside the words: *Whitetail, Montana*.

Guess I did cross into Montana.

He tosses my bag in the backseat and opens the passenger side door for me, offering his hand to help me inside.

Broody *and* chivalrous. What a combination.

Reluctantly taking his hand, I hold it tight so my boot doesn't slip off the icy running board. The heat from his rough, calloused fingers is insanely soothing in a way that says, *I've got you*—and I'd love nothing more than to curl up on his hands alone. They're just *that* warm.

And I'm just *that* desperate for human contact.

Get it together, Maci, this is a stranger.

I mumble a quiet *thanks*, and he closes the door. He jogs to the driver's side, hops in and immediately turns up the heat. He takes the truck out of park, and a steady rumble starts down the road.

I tug my seatbelt on, glancing around the new-to-me space. It's suspiciously clean—for a working man's truck—but smells like male musk, oil, and fuel. It's kind of nice, actually. And coming from this pregnant nose with heightened senses, it's a compliment.

"How long were you out there for?" he asks.

I peer around curiously while trying to get a sense if I'm being led to a quieter area to be murdered. "Half hour, maybe." There are a few scattered tools in the back I take note of, a larger wrench that I could easily crack him on the head with if I need to get away. "Why?"

"Your hands are like ice," he growls, turning up the heat even higher. "You warming up over there?"

"I'm okay," I say, watching his every move as he checks his phone and comes to a stop on the side of the road a few minutes later.

He makes a call, sparing me a glance before looking away. "Hey, Joey. Listen I've got a white SUV dead out here on 237 heading north right in the dead zone. Yeah, I'm gonna need a tow. No, I want it done now. I don't give a fuck. We'll be here waiting so try not to dick around, asshole." Duke sighs. "Yeah, all right, see ya in a bit."

He hangs up and tosses the phone in the cup holder, rubbing his face roughly. "Might be a while," he says, "Friday night an all."

I'm not sure what that has to do with getting my car towed, but... "Is there, um, a motel in this town?" I ask.

Duke turns to me, his dark eyes making his intense gaze harsher as he glares at me. "Do you have any idea where the hell you even are, lady?"

I narrow my eyes at him. How did we go from *ma'am* to *lady* so quickly? "My GPS stopped working a while ago, I thought I was still in Wyoming," I admit, fishing out my phone from my pocket. "And my name is *Maci*. Maci Baker."

He scoffs. "The border between Wyoming and Montana is probably a good four hours back. How the hell do you not know where you are? Do you have any idea how unsafe that—"

"Yes," I snap, hot tears stinging my eyes for the third time in the last hour. I put a protective hand over my belly at the nauseating wave of emotion that sweeps over me. "I do know, and if you could stop making me feel like crap about it, that'd be far more helpful than whatever it is you're doing now."

I've had a rough four weeks with no one in my corner for any of it, the last thing I need is this jerk reading me the riot act.

His gaze lingers on my hand and his brow furrows as I slowly slide it back to my side. The dry air blasting from the vents feels twenty degrees hotter in this tense silence.

When he finally locks eyes with me once again, there's a glimmer of hurt in them that wasn't there a moment ago.

And I can't help the pain in my heart that follows.

Who the hell is this guy?

Three.

Duke

I STUDY HER—THIS *MACI Baker*. If there ever was a name to fit this woman more perfectly, it'd be that.

Stunning emerald eyes paired with long, deep red hair cascading in subtle waves out of the dark grey beanie she has on and down well past her chest. Freckles bridge over her nose from cheek to cheek above full, plump lips with a delicate jawline that has me fighting to keep my hands to myself.

I don't think I've ever met anyone as pretty as she is.

The flimsy black coat she has on can't be doing shit for her on this winter night being below freezing—without factoring in the windchill. She's got on black yoga pants and grey winter boots with faux fur around the top. And from what I could see when she got in the truck, she's got a body to match those lips and tight ass.

"All right, well…" What else can I offer her to be more *helpful* than I already am? "Did you want to call your husband before we head back into the dead zone? I'm sure he'd want to know you're okay."

I sure as shit would if my woman was this gorgeous, I think to myself, then hate myself for the thought even crossing my mind. *You don't have a woman, moron. You're alone, remember?*

How could I forget?

"I…don't have a husband," she tells me.

I raise a brow. "Boyfriend? Girlfriend?"

She shakes her head, and it's unclear if the blasting heat is getting to me or if I like that bit of information more than I should.

"Where you heading, Maci?" I try to contain the thump in my chest from saying her name aloud and how good it sounds when I do.

Who the hell is this chick?

"Currently…" she trails off with a vague gesture around the truck. "Wherever you're willing to take me."

"I'll take you wherever you want," I say, and it's the truth. "Where were you goin' before?"

"Anchorage."

My eyes widen. "Alaska?"

She pains a laugh. "Yeah, I don't expect you to take me that far, but a cheap motel would work for now."

"That I can do," I say, and she nods.

We fall into a sort of amicable silence that *should* be awkward as hell—but it's not.

When I catch her covering her mouth to yawn, I ask, "You sure you'd rather wait here? I can tell ya Joey's trustworthy, and I'll have him back your car into the shop where it'll be safe." Thankfully one of the three bays I cleared out earlier is still open—which is a rarity these days.

Maci chews her lip. "You, um, said there was a storm coming in. Do you know when?"

"Soon," I admit, not wanting to scare her, but also not wanting to be out here if we don't need to be. "Supposed to last through the night." She shifts uncomfortably, and I tap my thumb on the steering wheel. "I doubt anyone is going to be out driving around knowing it's hitting tonight. We can turn back and get whatever you need from your car before I take you to the local motel."

She looks around for the tenth fuckin' time. Am I *that* intimidating? I mean, sure, she's in a vulnerable position at the moment, but I hope I don't look like someone who'd hurt her.

"Okay," she says quietly, nerves evident in her soft tone. "I already have what I need, so, um, can you take me to the motel?"

I shift the truck out of park. "You got it."

We head off toward town. The ride is silent again as Maci gazes out the window, likely gathering just how far out she was from town or even the nearest house.

"Thank you for stopping," she finally says, breaking the dreaded silence I've grown accustomed to—not by choice.

"Don't mention it," I say, clearing my throat. "So, what's in Alaska?"

"Snow," she quips at me with a giggle. I grin at the airy light sound. She leans her head back against the headrest, hugging into herself with a heavy sigh. "Have you ever just wanted to go somewhere where no one knows your name? No one knows your story..."

My chest tightens. Yes. Fuck, yes, I do.

"That's in Alaska," she adds. "If I ever make it there."

"Where were you coming from?"

"Oklahoma."

I scoff. "Christ, you're lucky you made it this far. Your transmission looks like it's been dying for a while with that oil pan fucked, I'm surprised you didn't blow the entire engine."

Maci's nose scrunches adorably. "It's really bad, isn't it?"

"Well, I'll need to get under it, take a good look, but she's not going to be a cheap fix. And finding a transmission isn't going to be a cakewalk either. Probably take a week to get between the storm and shortages. Tack on another few days to go through the motions before you're up and running again."

"Oh." Her voice is straining as I glance at her, the tears already welling in her eyes when she asks, "Do you know a ballpark on how much all that might cost?"

"Hard to say," I grunt. "It'll depend on the transmission and pan cost, but you're looking at over three grand without labor."

She drops her head in her hands, whispering, "Shit."

"You'll have the weekend to figure out what you want to do," I say. "I'll call around Monday, get you a quote priced out, then we'll go from there."

At her silence, my gaze drifts to her with a hand over her stomach. Eyes closed and taking in slow, steady breaths. A split second later, her eyes snap open, and she covers her mouth with a heave. "Pull over," she chokes out, her body leaning forward like she's about to puke.

"Ah, fuck," I bite out, slamming on the brake and pulling off to the side of the road.

Maci swings the door open, nearly collapsing into the snowbank. I throw my truck in park and jump out, racing to her side. I come up behind her as she clings to the open door, throwing up right in the snow. I reach for her, holding her hair back even as she tries to wave me off. I don't listen, finding myself rubbing her back with my free hand.

She throws up a few more times before she catches her breath enough to stand upright. I release her hair, grab a handful of napkins from the center console, and hand them to her. "Here."

"Thank you," she sniffles, wiping her mouth and hands.

I try not to grimace when I notice... "Your coat."
She looks down.

"Could this day get any worse?" she mutters, wiping and smearing the bit of vomit from her coat.

I don't think twice as I grab a fistful of snow, using the hunk of ice to wipe off the bottom of her coat. Maci tenses at my actions, and I don't blame her—this is out of pocket from one stranger to another. But I *have* to do something for her right now.

I chuck the snow in the ditch and take a napkin from her hand before wiping my own. "Take off your coat," I grunt. She just looks at me strangely as I take off my jacket and toss it on the front seat. I tug my hoodie over my head and hand it to her. "Put this on."

Her gaze is locked on the extended offering. "I'm okay."

I scowl. Is she going to argue with me at every turn? "Your coat is wet. Take it off and put this on before we both freeze out here."

She huffs, gracing me with an emerald glare before unzipping her flimsy excuse of a coat and revealing the body of a goddamn goddess. Hourglass curves are prominent in her tight, light grey long-sleeve, showing off a bodacious chest that matches her pouty-plump lips and ass.

Fuckin' hell, woman.

She hands me her coat and takes the hoodie, quickly dragging it over her head. I shake out her damp coat and hang it in the backseat on a hook, then yank back on my heavy jacket. "You good now?"

Maci folds the droopy sleeves over her chest, hugging herself as she stares down at *my* hoodie that looks far too good where it falls well past her ass and hangs loosely around her. "Yes, thank you."

I nod, helping her into the truck. I don't bother trying to ignore the extra thump in my chest over seeing this woman wearing the hoodie right off my back as I stride around the truck and get in.

I'm a nice guy, I attempt to reason with myself, it has nothing to do with...her.

I offer her the half-drank bottle of water sitting between us and grin when she makes a face at it. "Sorry, it's all I got."

She tentatively takes the water and opens it, giving it a sniff and shake while eyeing the contents. "It's from earlier today." I chuckle. "I'm not diseased and I didn't drug it."

Maci rolls her eyes with a small smile. "I didn't say anything," she mutters, pouring a little into her mouth and swishing it around before lowering the window and spitting it out.

Satisfied, I start us back down the road for town. "You feelin' better over there?" I ask after a few minutes.

She rubs her stomach. "Yes. I'm sorry for the, uh, jump scare." She laughs lightly. "Must have been that gas station food from a few hours ago."

I eye her skeptically. *Is she lying to me?*

And why does the thought bother me so fuckin' much?

"Thank you for holding my hair, though."

"No problem," I grunt, turning down the main street that leads to my shop. I point ahead. "That's the shop," I say as she follows the cue with those pretty eyes. "Wanted you to at least see where it is so you'll know where your car will be. The motel is right up the way here," I add. "There's a diner down the street and a coffee shop that's pretty good."

I turn into the motel parking lot right out front of the office door. "I'll wait here for you."

"Okay." She smiles, grabs her purse, and slides out. She scurries into the main office of The Whitetail Motel, the wind whipping as the snow starts to fall in fat, heavy flakes.

I keep my eyes on her even as my phone rings. "Hey," I answer, not paying any mind to who's calling.

"What's goin' on?" Butch asks. "You home?"

"Not yet," I huff, failing to keep the irritation out of my voice. It's been a week since he and Cassidy made their little announcement to the family, and I'm not proud to say, I've been avoiding my brother like he's carrying the plague. "Came across a car dead on the side of the road."

"Everything good there?"

I take in a deep breath, my focus remaining on Maci as she signs off for her room and takes the old-fashioned, brass key from the attendant. "Yeah, I'm taking care of it."

"Well, I'll make this quick," he starts. "Cass wants to do a night out tomorrow. Dinner at Red's, then over to Tavern Nine. They're doing country night, and since her birthday is mid-week, she wants to celebrate early."

"I'll be there," I say, and I mean it. Regardless of whatever inner bullshit turmoil I've got swimming around in my head, I'm not *that* big of an asshole.

Butch is quiet for a long moment.

"Is that all?"

"I haven't heard from you since Sunday," he grumbles.

"Yeah, well, I've been busy."

"Duke," he bites out. "I'm your goddamn brother. You can't avoid the inevitable, man."

Maci pushes open the glass office door, jumping as the wind takes it from her and slams into the building. My body tenses at the urge to leap out and help her.

I tighten my hold on the steering wheel in front of me. What the hell is wrong with me tonight? I need to *stop* this—whatever it is I'm doing. *She can walk the twenty feet by herself.*

I huff as Maci waves an apology to the attendant before battling the wind to close the door and get to the truck.

"I'm not avoiding shit, all right?" It's a blatant lie I don't plan on admitting anytime soon. "I've gotta go. I'll see y'all tomorrow."

As I hang up, Maci opens the door, hoisting herself up to hop into the truck. "They had one room left," she beams, brushing hair out of her flushed, wind-whipped face with a smile. "They said it's on the end. Room sixteen."

I drive to the end of the lot and park in front of the motel room door. I get out and make my way to her side. She slides out as I open the back door and gather her coat and bag.

She reaches for the bag. "I can take—"

"I got it." I tip my chin to the door for her to move ahead and open it.

"I didn't know motels still had these keys," she says, pushing inside.

The room is basic—a king bed centered against the wall, two nightstands, a dresser across from the bed with a TV on top, a small table with two chairs, and an attached bathroom. It's nothing to write home about, but it's clean.

She flicks a light switch, illuminating the room in a soft glow from the bedside lamps. I set her bag and coat on the table, then head for the floor heater beneath the window.

Is this thing even on? It's freezing in here.

"Oh, they said the heat is a little off in here," she tells me as I crouch in front of the vents that are barely blowing out what I'd consider *heat*. "They gave me a discount for tonight. I guess someone is coming to fix it tomorrow."

I smack my palm on the side of the heater and scowl. What the hell?

"Is there some kind of event going on out here?" she asks curiously. "All the other rooms were taken and the parking lot is pretty full. Is it always like this?"

"There's a ski resort on the mountain. Hot vacation spot for tourists," I say, smacking the heater again and earning a burst of air blown in my face. "A lot can't afford to stay at the resort hotel, so they stay in town." The heater makes an awful rattle and slows down. "Piece of shit."

Maci giggles behind me and I face her. "Is it going to cost me extra if you fix the heat, too?"

I scoff, standing. "You going to be okay in here?"

"I'll be fine." She takes in a deep breath. "Thank you for...everything."

"Did you need anything else?" I ask, since I can't seem to help myself tonight. "I can run to the store or somethin' for ya. Food, water, whatever you need."

She smiles. "There's a gas station across the street, I'll walk over in a bit, but thank you for the offer."

My jaw tightens, not liking her response. Or the idea of her walking around this late at night alone. *She's not your responsibility, Duke, back off.*

But I can't.

"I'll drive you over."

"It's right across the street, don't worry about it," she says, grabbing her purse and slipping in the room key. "Matter of fact, I'll go now before the sidewalks get any more covered."

When she goes to take off my hoodie, I stop her. "Leave it on. Your coat is still wet."

"Are you sure? I can—"

"It's not like I don't know where you're going to be," I grunt. "Besides, it's probably warmer than that thin excuse of a coat you've got."

"It's not *that* thin," she mutters. I raise a brow. "Okay, fine, it's not exactly the best for keeping out wind, but it's still warm."

I open the door. "You ready?"

Her brow furrows as she watches me closely. "Don't you have somewhere else to be? Like going home to a significant other?"

The question digs at me even though I keep my voice free of emotion when I deadpan, "No."

As hard as I've ever tried to push away this feeling in my gut I've had for the last hour or more, I can't any longer. Because something is churning inside of me to make sure she's okay. Safe, warm, fed. Whether it's knowing she's stranded or alone—or fuckin' both.

I need to. For me.

Four.

Maci

Duke talked me back into his truck—well, more like demanded it. Then insisted he take me down the road to a grocery store where a bottle of water isn't the same price as a whole case. Thankfully, they were open for another ten minutes, giving me enough time to grab a case of water, a bundle of bananas, and a bag of chips.

"Are you hungry?" he asks, following me with the case of water in hand as I push us back into the chilly motel room.

I set my purse and grocery bag on the table with a sigh. "I'm fine."

"You keep saying that," he grinds out in clear frustration.

This guy is too much.

What does he expect me to say? That: No, I'm *not* fine. Yes, I *am* hungry. Or maybe he'd like to know how I've never felt more alone in my life than I do right now.

The very thought is enough to make me burst into tears.

"Hey, you all right?" he asks, closing the space between us in two long strides as I turn away.

When he lays a gentle hand on my back, I quickly wipe away the useless tears on his overly large, hoodie sleeves. When he took this off to give it to me, I was torn between pouncing on the man or drooling senseless. The way his tattered white T-shirt underneath started to ride up, exposing a set of thick, taut muscles patched with dark hair on his abdomen leading into the deepest V cut I've ever seen.

I bet he could—*Stop it, Maci.*

These damn pregnancy hormones. I swear it's turning me into some harlot. Not that that's a bad thing, of course.

I blow out an exaggerated breath in an attempt to reel my emotions in check.

"Do you know anyone in Montana?" His voice is low, comforting, and filled with concern. When I turn to him, he's watching me. Sharp brown eyes appearing almost caramel in the soft glow from the nearby lamp.

"No," I confess.

He nods, pulling out his wallet and fishing out a business card. "The second number is my personal cell. Send me a text now so I have your number, and I'll give you a call first thing

Monday morning." He slips the card between my fingers as I get my phone to do as he says. "If you need anything—and I mean, *anything*—you call me. Got it?"

I bite my lip to keep from smiling. The stern tone of his voice doesn't match the kindness behind his eyes. "Yes, sir," I tease.

He shakes his head with a crooked grin. "I'm serious, Maci."

Warmth spreads throughout my body. From my toes to my fingertips, I'm acutely aware of how close he is to me right now. "I know."

Seemingly satisfied with my response, Duke stalks over to the heater, smacking it again for good measure. "Well, at least it's blowing out something. You sure you'll be all right here?" he asks for the second time tonight, and I'm starting to get the impression he's reluctant to leave at all.

"Yes," I say. "And if I'm not, I know this bossy mechanic. I'm sure I could call him if I need anything." *Oh, lord, I'm flirting with this guy.*

His grin widens. "Sounds like a stand-up guy."

I shrug. "I don't know, he's pretty bossy so far."

He chuckles deeply, gesturing behind him with a jerk of his thumb. "All right, well, I'll let you get some rest." He points at my phone in hand. "Make sure you call that bossy mechanic if you need anything."

I smile. "I will."

When he leaves, I lock the door behind him and go to the window to tug the curtains closed, then pause. Duke hops in his truck, his gaze lifting to bore into me with an unreadable expression.

I suck in a breath and give a little awkward wave before closing the curtains.

I can't believe I just flirted with him. When all he did was be a complete gentleman, not a serial killer in the slightest, and here I am—hormonal and horny—wishing he'd toss me on this creaky motel bed and have his way with me.

I need to get it together.

I put a few things away before taking a long, hot shower then change into a pair of pajama pants, two pairs of socks, and another long sleeve. I reach for Duke's hoodie then hesitate, deciding against wearing it to bed.

I turn off the lights and flick on the TV to curl up under the covers. Shivering at the cold chill everything has on it, I wait for my body heat to do its job as my mind starts to rattle through the too-few options I have going forward.

I slip a hand out from my huddled mess of stiff sheets and a sorry excuse for a comforter to grab my phone. I swipe through, clicking on the schedule I made for myself, and realize I should be starting my new job one week from today. Except...if Duke is right, there's no way I'll make it there on time.

And I *begged* for the opportunity to open a yoga studio at their local fitness center. They gave it to me on the condition it was a short-term lease to *prove* I'd be a welcome addition to their business. Who knows what they'll say now if I can't meet the deadline...

Have I mentioned I'm on the unlucky streak of a lifetime?

I jump, my phone startling me with a text.

Duke: *Hey, just checking in.*

I smile.

Me: *All good here. Did you make it home okay?*

Duke: *Yeah.*

Duke: *It's getting pretty nasty out. If you lose power or think you need to head anywhere, let me know, and I'll come get you.*

Me: *Do you offer this kind of service to all your customers?*

Duke: *Only you.*

I bite my lip, snuggling down as I prepare to send off another message when—

Duke: *Let me know if you need anything. Night.*

I frown. I shouldn't be disappointed, I have no reason to be, and yet...I am. With another heavy sigh, I plug my phone in and turn off the TV to curl up in the hopes I'll be able to get some much-needed sleep *without* the image of a certain bossy mechanic in mind.

Between my shivering, the stiff bed, and the rattling heater—it's a wonder I was able to get two hours of sleep before two men started banging on my door at 7:00 AM sharp. They're *supposed* to be fixing the heater—or so they claim—but I haven't seen them do much of anything besides argue about what's wrong with the dang thing.

It's now after nine, and I'm curled up on the ice-cold linoleum floor of the bathroom, praying for my stomach to settle long enough so I can get dressed and walk to the diner Duke mentioned yesterday. Unfortunately, it's not looking good.

I clutch the bowl of the toilet as morning sickness takes control of my body for the fifth time. Starting the day off right, it seems. *Ugh*.

"Hey—"

"What's up—"

"Where is—"

Broken bits of conversation filter through the thin walls, and from the sounds of it, the two repairmen have called for reinforcements. How many men does it take to fix a motel-grade heater?

I snort.

One of the voices gets louder and almost...familiar? I strain my ears to listen.

"Maci?" A heavy fist bangs on the door, shaking the frame. I jolt. "Maci, it's me, Duke. Open up."

What's he doing here? Oh, no. Did something happen to my car? I knew we shouldn't have left it unlocked and vulnerable like he said.

I carefully scoot toward the door and reach up. The door swings inward, and Duke's gaze scans the tiny bathroom faster than I can blink before it settles on me at his feet. I can only imagine how pitiful I appear in my current state: hair tossed up on top of my head, zero makeup to cover the massive bags under my eyes I'm surely sporting, and pale—I bet I'm as pale as printer paper—with the stiff, ugly motel comforter wrapped loosely around me.

Yup. Lookin' like a solid twenty bucks right about now.

"Morning," I say, paining a smile.

His heavy brow furrows into deep concern as he crouches, assessing me. "What the hell are you doing on the floor?" he asks, the rough back of his hand coming to rest on my forehead as if I'm a sick child. "You don't look so good. Did you throw up again?"

I huff out a laugh. "Gee, thanks."

"We tried to tell her to leave," one of the repairmen shouts, speaking out of turn. Doesn't he know this is an A and B conversation?

Duke's jaw tightens, his focus solely on me. "Why didn't you call me?"

I tilt my head in confusion. Is he mad at me? "Why would I? You said only if I needed something."

"Yeah, and your lips are blue, Maci," he bites out. "You're cold as ice and from the looks of it, I should be taking you to the hospital." He stands, gently pressing the door open farther as he steps into my space. "Come on." He reaches for me like he's about to hoist me up by my underarms.

I swat him away. "I don't need a hospital."

"She's been barfin' in there all morning," another moron calls out unhelpfully.

Can no one mind their own business around here?

Duke's gaze darkens. "We're going," he grits, picking me up and off the floor with ease despite an extra swat to his chest. "I'll help you get ready. What do you—"

"Duke," I hiss under my breath, "I don't need a doctor."

"Yes, you do," he growls.

"No, I don't," I growl back.

"Something is clearly wrong," he says, his eyes darting over me, the room, the toilet.

"I'm—" The words lodge in my throat. I haven't told anyone about my, um, *situation*. To be blunt, no one besides my doctor back in Oklahoma knows I'm pregnant. I never had the chance to tell my family or friends before everything blew up in my face. And the only person I did tell...well, he's dead.

Not exactly on a winning streak for announcements.

Duke eases the door shut behind him. "If you're worried about going alone, I'll stay with you," he says softly with so much sincerity I believe him.

I shake my head. "It's not that..."

"Hospitals are scary, I get it," he adds, trying a different angle as he tugs the comforter up and off the floor to wrap tighter around me. "This one time, my brother Levi super-glued his boxers on his head—well, I think Butch might have done it to him, but that's beside the point."

"Duke." I smile, laying a hand on his arm. "I'm not afraid of hospitals or doctors, I just don't need one."

"This isn't normal, Maci." He frowns, searching my face for an answer. "Do you think it's food poisoning? Stress? It could be the flu…"

"Duke."

"…you're probably dehydrated. I can run to the store, get you some Pedialyte."

"Duke."

"My mom is a nurse; I'll call her and—"

"I'm pregnant." The words are out before I can stop them, and I gasp at my outburst. The sound echoes in the tight, unwelcoming location. My heart hammers in my chest as I watch his frozen, shell-shocked face.

At least he isn't yelling.

And why would he? I shouldn't care what this man-stranger-whoever thinks about my pregnancy. It's mine, not his.

"You're…" His hand rubs over his brow and down the side of his scruffy face then over his mouth. "That explains a lot."

I bite my lip and nod, averting my eyes out of…shame? Embarrassment? Guilt? It's anyone's guess. "Yup."

His frame expands on a deep breath, and I'm acutely aware of how intimidating he is in his same attire as last night—with a new black hoodie in place of the one he lent me. All rugged and strong, he exudes masculinity, and I feel very, *very* small under his intense scrutiny.

I'd give anything to know what he's thinking.

"What do you need from me?"

That's...unexpected. I'm not sure I follow. "What do you mean?"

"I mean, how am I supposed to help you," he says, sounding so vulnerable it makes my heart ache. "I can't leave you here...like this. It's a damn meat locker in your room. Not that it's much better in here by any means. You were sick last night, and you have been all morning. You're here all by yourself, and now you tell me you're...ya know." *Boy, do I know.* "I won't leave you."

His last four words have me in a chokehold.

He didn't mean it like that, you thirsty woman. It doesn't matter how he meant it, I needed to hear it all the same. Whether it's the last month catching up to me or the flood of hormones my body's tirelessly creating, I burst into tears on the spot.

Duke guides me into his strong embrace without a word, and I cling to him like the sad sack I am. He shushes me in a soft, deep tone that has me melting. "It's all right, doll."

A broken, choked laugh escapes me, and I lean away, wiping my damp face on the comforter then promptly cringe at the action. He grabs a tissue from the counter and hands it to me. "Thank you," I sniffle. "Sorry, I'm not usually like this."

He leans back against the door, watching me with those avid eyes that don't seem to miss a thing. "I figured that." He grins. "Hormones and whatnot. They say it makes a woman crazy."

My gaze snaps to him with a glare. "I am *not* crazy."

Hormonal, yes. Crazy? No.

He chuckles, lifting his hands in mock surrender. "I never said you were," he says, eyeing me as I shuffle closer to the sink. "Did you eat yet?"

I shake my head, splashing water on my face and dabbing it dry with a fresh towel. "No, I've been in here since those repair guys got here at seven."

In the reflection of the mirror, Duke's expression goes from playful to sour in point-two seconds. I turn to him. "What?"

"Wait here," he grunts, spinning on his heel and whipping the door open with more force than I would. He storms out without another word. I close the door with a light click behind him. *Okay...*

Shouting ensues from outside the door, and it doesn't take long for me to realize Duke's kicking out the repairmen with some seriously heated threats. Like 'endangering the welfare' of...me, I suppose.

"You let her sit there freezing for over two fucking hours!"

"Hey, man, we're just trying to do our job here."

"Get the fuck out. *Now*." Duke's tone is downright violent. It sends an all-too-pleasant shiver between my thighs that I can't help if I cared to try. And I don't.

The heavy slam of the outer door rattles the flimsy bathroom one. I turn the knob slowly and peer out with caution. Duke is in the middle of the room, cleaning up the several screws and worn panels the two men removed from the heater.

"Is it safe to come out?" I ask teasingly, except the look Duke gives me is anything but lighthearted.

He picks up the small pieces and kicks the rest to the side. "Do whatever you gotta do to get ready," he says. "I'll go talk to someone at the front desk about getting this taken care of. Then we'll head to breakfast."

He doesn't give me a chance to respond otherwise before he's out the door—where a dusting of snow has drifted in to layer the flat, rough carpeting in white ice. I stand there for a minute, a bit confused and a tad more conflicted on following his lead—or should I say, *orders*—before my stomach gurgles in pain, and I remember, I'm eating for two.

And Duke's company over a blueberry muffin or three does sound tempting.

Five.

Duke

I LINGER IN THE front office as I absently listen to the owner apologize to Maci for the heating issue and his *nephews'* disrespect. He offers her a full refund for the night and an extension on her stay until Thursday.

Which is the longest she can be here since the room is booked and paid for by another customer. And I don't miss the uncomfortable fidget in her posture when she learns this.

Mentally, I'm working out how I can get her car fixed and back to her in record time to alleviate any kind of stress she's already under. Even though I *know* it'll be the better part of a week at minimum.

If she needs somewhere to stay, she can stay with me.

The thought heats my chest in a way it hasn't in years. Would she go for that? Can I get her to trust me enough by then to have her safely tucked away at the cabin?

Safely. What has gotten into me?

She's silent as we walk across the parking lot to my truck. I help her inside and jog around to jump in the driver's seat. "You should've called," I grumble for the third time, earning me a shake of her head as I turn up the heat for her. I don't know *why* I keep drilling this into her; it's annoying even from my perspective.

"I'll keep that in mind for next time."

My jaw tightens. There better not be a next time. "My brother, Rhett, knows a good bit about electrical heaters," I say. "I gave him a call, but he can't get out here for another hour or two. In the meantime, you can tag along with me until your room heats up."

"Tag along...with you," she repeats, confused. And I don't blame her.

"I'm not sending you into that meat locker of a motel room, Maci," I say, rubbing the back of my neck. It feels tighter with her in my truck wearing my hoodie under her flimsy jacket. You wouldn't know she's been up for hours with...morning sickness. My chest expands at the thought yet again, and I push it down. *Way* down. "I've got some errands to run and plowing to do. You'll be safer—uh, *warmer*, in my truck."

Get your shit together, man. Fuck.

"Fine." She sighs, tugging on her seatbelt. "Can we still eat first?"

A genuine grin splits my face. "Absolutely."

We set on the short drive down the road to Annie's Diner, passing Cup O' Joe on the way. I catch sight of Butch's truck along with half a dozen other vehicles I recognize all too well parked out front. Vehicles that usually hang out at Annie's Diner this early on a Saturday...

I slow our approach when an abandoned Buick—half in the street—sits blocking the unplowed entrance to the restaurant. Where another local plow guy is working to get the car unstuck and out of the way.

"Son of a—"

Maci leans forward to get a better look at the scene. "Should we wait?"

I mull it over for a second, but the answer is clear. I can't make her wait to eat when I can hear her stomach growling from a few feet away. No matter how badly *I* don't want to walk into Cup O' Joe, the thought of her not eating in the next half-hour doesn't sit right with me.

"No," I grunt, checking the side mirror before I whip a U-turn. "We'll just hit the coffee shop, if that's all right with you," I say, glancing at her.

She nods, smiling sheepishly. "I am craving a muffin."

As irritated as I am at having to deal with Butch this morning, I can't deny the joy I get knowing I'm giving her something she wants. Even if it is fulfilling a minor craving.

However, the second we pull into the tightly packed parking lot, Butch is walking out the front door. *If I could've stalled another thirty seconds, we would've missed him.* Damn.

My brother's stern gaze locks on me like a viper eyeing his enemy. This ought to be fun.

I kill the engine and get out, standing by the front of my truck as Maci slides out.

A few long strides later and Butch is within arm's reach. "How's it going?"

"Good," I huff, my breath clouding between us. Maci shuffles her way to my side, doing a light hop in an attempt to ward off the bitter cold.

Butch's gaze catches on her, and I can only imagine what's going through his thick skull. Beautiful girl slides out of my truck first thing in the morning wearing my hoodie from last night on our way in to grab breakfast.

I know *exactly* how this looks.

Maci glances between Butch and myself. "I'll, um, find us a table," she whispers to me, touching my arm before giving an uncomfortable, tightlipped smile to my brother and scurrying in the front door.

Butch wastes no time in asking, "Who is she?"

"A friend."

"Friend, huh?"

I narrow my gaze into a harsh warning that could rival any Butch Montgomery scowl tenfold. "That's what I said."

He pushes his hands in his pockets, and I'd love nothing more than to knock the skeptical glare off his face. He can try to play 'big bro' all he wants, we both know I can kick his ass if it came down to it. "You still plan on showing up tonight?" he asks in a condescending tone. *Prick.*

"I said I would, didn't I?"

"You also said you'd be the Montgomery to die alone on this mountain," he adds, tipping his head in the direction of the coffee shop. "Seems you changed your mind pretty fast on that, too."

Bastard always knows how to kick a man when he's down. "Fuck off," I mutter as I stalk past him. I throw open the heavy glass-framed door and step inside the bustling local coffee house.

I find Maci a second later, standing fifth in line. I come up beside her, laying a gentle hand on her lower back. She jumps, staring up at me with those pretty, expressive eyes. I wonder if she knows how much she gives away in them.

"Everything okay?" she asks quietly.

I nod.

"There's no open tables," she adds, peering around.

"We can take it to go," I say, my gaze trained ahead, jaw ticking. There are at least a dozen sets of eyes on us even now, and I hate it. I hate the whispers that'll be flying around by noon. And I hate that Maci, the stranger in town seen with the broken widower who hasn't been on a date in years, will be at the center of it.

She has no idea the shit she just got dropped into.

"Oh, okay." She fidgets beside me, her arm brushing against mine. "So, um, were you just in the area this morning, or did something happen with my car?" she asks.

"I was on my way to the shop and saw your door wide open," I admit, not adding that I had to take the long way around to pass the motel to check on her. "Your car got in safe and sound last night. We can check on it if you don't believe me."

She worries on her lower lip as we move up in line. "No, that's all right."

Five minutes later, we're stepping up to the register. "Hey, Duke," Cassidy beams, her smile blinding as her eyes widen at the sight of Maci standing close. "You just missed Butch."

Unfortunately, I didn't. "Caught him outside," I say, gesturing for Maci to order. She gets two blueberry muffins, a green tea, and a small coffee while I grab a breakfast sandwich, an apple-cinnamon muffin, and the biggest coffee I can get to go.

I didn't get much sleep last night. The whole night I spent watching my phone like a hawk, worried I was going to miss her call or text. If I didn't know any better, I'd say I even missed her. *Fuck.* I missed a woman I know *nothing* about besides the fact she's gorgeous and stranded alone in a town she didn't know the name of less than twelve hours ago.

Oh, and she's...pregnant.

And single. Can't forget that.

What kind of sick joke is this? *Is it a* joke *or a* sign?

A delicate hand on my arm drags me from the thought just in time. "I'll be right back," Maci tells me.

My heart thuds in fear for no reason at all. I'm not thinking as I wrap an arm around her, pull her to me, and search her gaze. "Why? What's wrong?" The very fragment of a thought the cold from earlier could've harmed her or the baby... I can't even think about it without wanting to rip those two idiots to shreds.

Her cheeks blush a deep enough red to match her hair. "I have to pee," she whispers.

"Oh." The tightness in my shoulders ease and I drop my arm from her waist. Way to jump to the worst-case scenario. "Right, well, the bathroom is over there." I point to the narrow hallway near the back.

She smiles with a shake of her head as she slips past me. I keep an eye on her longer than I should, glaring at Don Mays as he leans to get a better look at her ass. His leer lifts at my heated stare. The moron gives me a thumbs-up before looking elsewhere. Asshole.

"She's pretty," Cassidy says, setting down two brown paper bags and a disposable tray of drinks on the counter between us. I grunt, fishing out my wallet as she rattles off the price. "I didn't know you were...on the market."

"What?"

"Dating," she clarifies.

"I'm not," I deadpan. Why does everything have to be about my love life? Or lack thereof.

She shrugs. "Well, you're welcome to invite her to the bar tonight after dinner," she says. "The more the merrier."

I'd like to say the idea hadn't already crossed my mind, but it has. I've caught myself thinking of ways I can help her—*protect* her. It's probably one of the more primitive urges I've ever had.

Again, I ask, *What the hell is going on with me?*

When Maci returns to me, there's a lightness I feel when I'm around her that I can't deny—even despite the prying eyes surrounding us. It replaces the dark cloud that's been fogging my mind these last few years with...her.

It's dangerous, this feeling.

And I've already become addicted.

Six.

Duke

Maci shimmies off her coat and tucks it in the backseat before slipping off her boots. She delicately folds her feet beneath her in the passenger seat, taking her hot tea between her hands and holding it close to her chest. "So, where to?" she says with a smile, blowing on her steaming drink in a way that does things to me I'm not proud of.

Focusing my attention on the road, I shift my thickening cock as subtly as I can. "We'll be making the rounds first."

"Rounds?"

I grin. "Snow plowing."

"Ah, gotcha."

I back out onto the road and head east. The jolt of a pothole jostles her drink in hand causing a few drops to fall on her pants. I chuckle when she swipes it with the sleeve of my sweater.

"There are napkins in the glovebox," I tell her.

Her caught expression is both hilarious and adorable. "Sorry," she says. "You probably don't want me using it for clean-up purposes."

"Use it however you want." I grin. "I'm just letting you know."

She smiles, taking a sip of her tea as we head toward the property.

My phone pings with a text and I tug it free from my coat pocket, handing it to her. "Can you check that for me?" I spare a glance in her direction and note her surprised expression.

She gingerly takes my phone, clearing her throat as she swipes the screen to open. "No password?" she asks under her breath.

I shrug. "Never needed one."

Her gaze trails over me for a moment before refocusing on the screen. "It's your mom. She said the plow fell off your dad's truck, and she wants to know if you can come get her out of the driveway so she can go to the store while he *messes with the hunk of junk.*"

Of course, it did. "Tell her I'm heading to the property to plow for Levi to get up there, then I'll swing by."

She taps on the screen. "Is that spelled L-E-V-I, like the jeans?"

I chuckle at that. "Yeah."

"I might be from Oklahoma, but I've never heard that one," she muses, hitting send and setting the phone on the center console. "Who's Levi?"

"One of my brothers."

She raises a curious brow. "How many siblings do you have? You mentioned a Rhett earlier."

"Well, let's see…there's my eldest brother, Butch. He's the grumpy prick you saw outside the coffee shop," I start as she laughs. "He owns *Montgomery Logging*. Been doing pretty well for himself the last few seasons. I'm the second oldest. Then there's Beau, he's a few years younger than me. He's enlisted in the Army currently, and has two vacation cabin rentals on the mountain for extra income. And Rhett, he just turned thirty this year. He and Levi own and operate *Montgomery Lumber & Construction* together."

"Wow, you're all entrepreneurs," she says. "Your parents must be proud."

I snort. "Think there's a difference between being an entrepreneur and not wanting to work for some other asshole."

She giggles. "True."

"And last we've got a younger sister, Lily. She's twenty-five with a three-year-old son named Parker," I add. "She's living at home with our parents while she tries to get her modeling career started up again, or whatever—no one knows what the hell she's doing half the time."

"Four brothers and a sister. Oof." Maci cringes. "Your mother must be a saint to raise six kids."

She is. "That too many?"

"I mean, for me, yeah."

"How many do you want?" I ask without thinking.

"Well, I'd love three. That's kind of the dream, anyway," she says. "What about you? Do you want kids?"

I simply nod, not having the words on that one.

I did. I do. It's complicated.

"How many?" she presses.

"I've never put a number on it," I admit. "However many my woman would want, really."

"Well, I hope you at least have a max." She laughs. "I'm sure one of your parents put a cap on it at some point."

I chuckle deeply. "Yeah, I think they were aiming lower, but Ma wanted a daughter. Of course, sixth time was the charm."

Shaking her head, she says, "Five older brothers, I can't imagine."

I grin. You'd think, from the outside looking in, that Lily got the short end of the stick. Not the case. She's the baby and the only daughter—she's had our parents wrapped tight around her finger since day one without even trying.

"What about you, any siblings?"

Maci rolls her eyes. "I have an older sister, Tami. She's a real bitch."

"That bad, huh?"

"Oh, you have no idea," she adds dramatically. "She might as well be Satan's bride with the felon of a husband she chose for herself. He stole my car once. Had everyone convinced I said he could borrow it—obviously, I didn't. Yet, my entire family adores him. It's mind-blowing, if you ask me."

"What, uh, about you?" I force myself to ask, desperate to know. "You divorced? Doing the whole single mom thing."

"No, I've...never been married," she confesses, and my brow furrows. *How the hell is a woman like her not hitched by now?* "And yes, I'm doing the whole single mom thing. My ex didn't want anything to do with me or the baby. So, yeah, it's just us."

"I'm sorry," I say, internally stewing over her ex wanting nothing to do with his child. What kind of man does that?

"Don't be." She waves me off. "I don't have to worry about him anymore. Me and my baby can have a fresh start."

"That's a good way to think of it."

I slow as we reach the worn driveway leading to my property. I drop the plow and turn to start clearing the way. We hit a few bigger bumps, jerking the truck around. Maci yelps in shock, followed by a burst of laughter. I grin from ear to ear seeing her holding onto the door and console to stay in place.

"Hold on," I chuckle, continuing up the long, bumpy drive to the finished pole barn that'll act as my home garage alongside the half-built house. Rhett and Levi were able to get the foundation set, the frame of the house built, sheathing done, and the roof put on, all before the first snowfall of the season. Getting that far in the job when they did, left them able to work in the meantime on the inside.

"Whose house is this?" Maci asks, leaning forward to look up at the bare bones of a two-story house that'll hopefully end up being a three-bedroom, two-bath with a wraparound porch.

"Mine," I say, throwing the truck in park. "Rhett and Levi handle renovation projects, add-ons, and basic home builds." Pointing down the road. "Butch lives up the road with his fiancée. Roughly five miles past that is my folks' place. And down the road from them is where Beau's property starts. I'm renting one of his cabins while I wait on the build here."

Maci is quiet for a long moment. "So, you're pretty close with your family, huh?"

"When they're not up my ass half the time, yeah," I scoff. "My parents hold Sunday dinner every week, but we see each other often. Hang out a good bit. You close with your family?"

Her face scrunches in a slight cringe before she quickly masks it. "No, um, like I said, it's just me."

I nod. Getting the feeling I might be upsetting her, I change the subject. "Did you want to see the place?" I ask. "I usually do a quick walk-through, make sure no critters are taking up residence."

Her eyes light up, a beautiful smile on her full lips. "I'd love to."

"All right." I grin. "Just be careful getting out. This part of the driveway has a slope and—You know what, wait, I'll come around," I tell her, hearing her faint laughter as I get out and close the door behind me.

I stride around to her side and open the door. She pulls her jacket on, a humorous glint in her eye. "You know I'm not made of glass, right?" she teases.

I reach my hand out to help her down. "You are to me," I say, my heart stuttering at the admission. "I don't know what kind of falls a pregnant woman can take, but I don't plan on finding out."

She smiles, placing her delicate hand in mine. I keep hold of her hand, loving the fit, the feel, the beat of her pulse against mine. We walk hand in hand up the slight slope to the front steps. I release her hand only to grab the snow shovel propped against the railing.

"Does the porch go all the way around?" she asks, watching me shovel off the steps.

"Yeah," I grunt, setting the shovel off to the side and reaching for her hand again. For a split second, I think about dropping my hand. After all, the porch is covered, and the steps are clear. There's no *reason* for me to hold onto her.

Maci doesn't seem to question it, though. She takes my hand as we ascend the steps and I open the front door, gesturing her ahead of me. A wave of curiosity hits me at showing her my future home—the layout, the plan. I shouldn't care what she thinks. She's a perfect stranger, stuck here by the fault of her car.

She'll be gone before I know it.

Why does that sound so...painful?

I go through the motions of showing her the entire place. Explaining the divisions of the rooms by the bare framing for the walls, the open concept I'm aiming for on the first floor.

She engages in everything I say, asking small questions, and commenting on how amazing the view is from the kitchen that faces out over the mountain and surrounding forest.

"So, yeah. That's it so far," I finally say once we return to the entryway.

Maci turns away from admiring the stone fireplace in the living room. "Thanks for giving me the early tour."

"Anytime." I grin, gesturing to the door. "You ready?"

She takes my hand as I lead us out the way we came. Closing the door behind me, I glance up to see my brother pulling in beside the barn. Her grip on my hand loosens when she sees him, but I hold tight. Half not wanting her to slip, and the other not wanting to let go.

The majority being the latter.

Levi hops out, beaming his signature boyish smirk and looking like an idiot for not shaving that damn mustache yet. "Hey, bro. 'Bout time you plowed this," he says, then points to Maci like he's five. "Who's this?"

Levi and Rhett look a lot alike. Similar to Butch and I, they might as well be twins. Standing a few inches shorter than me, he's lean and broad, built for construction. He's growing out his hair and going through some 'mustache only' phase—looking like a seventies porn star if you ask me.

I shift my gaze to Maci pressed closer to me than she's been all day. My chest puffs out. "This is Maci," I say, not bothering to expand any more than that. "Maci, this is my younger brother, Levi."

Levi extends his hand. "Nice to meet you."

She shakes his hand with a cautious smile. "You, too."

He lifts his chin to the house at our backs. "I didn't know you were finally letting people in to check the place out," he says, sending me a slick wink. "What'd you think so far, Maci? Think Duke will fire us?"

"It looks great," she says. "I'm in love with the windows."

"Yeah, those were a bitch, but Duke insisted on the bigger ones with better insulation." My brother nods. "Better watch out, he's a tyrant to work with," he adds on a chuckle.

Maci peers up at me, biting her lip to keep from smiling too big. "He's pretty bossy, that's for sure."

I grin, squeezing her hand before turning my attention to Levi. "Did you talk to Rhett about those two-by-fours yet?"

"Yup, talked to him a few minutes ago. He needs you to sign off at the lumber yard before they close at two. Said he was at Whitetail Motel fixing a heater." He checks his phone. "Ma said you were stopping by to plow. Guess Dad's beater plow is done. About time, that thing is like a hundred years old."

I rub my chin. "Yeah, I better get over there."

Levi pulls out his keys and heads for the barn, yelling over his shoulder, "It was nice meeting you, Maci. I'll see you later at dinner, bro."

We're back in the truck and hitting the road toward my parents' house a few minutes later. "Sooo, does your brother do porn or something?" she asks.

"Fuck, no." I boom with laughter. "I'm glad I'm not the only one who sees it, though. He says it's *in* right now. Whatever that means, but I don't see it."

Maci giggles. "I mean, it kind of is? But I'm not so sure it's the way to go for him."

"I'll let him know you said that."

"No, you won't," she gasps, swatting my arm playfully. I throw my head back with a laugh. "Duke, don't you dare."

I chuckle deeply at her forced pout and the lingering play of a smile on her lips. Goddamn, even when she's pouting, she's stunning. "All right, all right," I give in. "I won't say anything...while you're still in town."

She laughs. "Well, don't hold your breath. I might be here a while."

I grin from ear to ear, liking the sound of that more and more by the minute. Maybe she'll even be willing to give me a chance...

Wait. Do I want a chance?

Seven.

Maci

DUKE PEELS OUT OF his parents' driveway, hitting the gas a little harder than necessary. I watch in the side mirror at—what I'm assuming is—his mother, trying to wave him down from their gorgeous, rustic farmhouse porch.

Seriously, this place is out of a magazine it's so breathtaking. Wrapped in classic Christmas décor—from the wreaths on every window to the white lights intertwined in garland—I'd love a picture if we weren't barreling in the opposite direction.

"I think she wants you to stop," I say, turning to Duke.

He grumbles under his breath, his hold on the wheel gripping a little tighter. I find myself staring at him with a flood of need between my thighs for not the first time today.

What is it with rugged men like him who can look sexy doing just about anything? They have no business turning women on with their competency. The way they use their palm to turn the steering wheel or stretch their arm over the back of the passenger seat when going in reverse.

Competency porn is *real*.

And my panties have been *melting* since last night.

Lay me out to dry if I ever see this man take out the trash without having to be asked.

"I'll see her tonight."

"Is it because of me?" I blurt out. *Subtle, Maci.*

I'd feel awful if I was causing a problem for him. I'm beyond grateful that he's the one who stopped to help me. Last night *and* this morning. He's one of the good ones. At least, from what I've seen. *I trust him*, I realize.

And the thought alone is enough to sober me from the stark fear of it. I haven't trusted anyone in a long, *long* time...

Duke rubs his face roughly, gaze darting between me and the road. "Do you want me to lie to you?"

"If you expect the truth from me, then I expect the truth from you." *Where'd that come from?*

He takes in a deep breath, blowing it out with his words, "Then yeah, it's because you're in here with me." My heart does a sad little dip despite myself. "It's nothing against you," he quickly adds, "I just know how she is, and there's been a few things going on... I don't want her reading me the riot act."

I raise a brow. "You left in a hurry because you didn't want to get yelled at by your mom?"

He scoffs. "When you say it like that, it sounds bad."

"How old are you again?" I laugh.

"What the hell does my age have to do with it?" He chuckles. "You've never gotten your ass chewed out by Julie Montgomery. Trust me, it ain't a pleasant experience."

His cell phone rings, and he checks the caller ID, then promptly ignores it, placing it on the center console.

"You're digging your grave deeper by pulling that move," I tell him.

"Hey, I'm driving." He grins. "Gotta keep my focus on the road, right?"

I yawn. "True."

"You holding up over there?" he asks. "Did you get any sleep last night?"

"I got some." I curl up on the seat, and cover my mouth to another yawn.

He eyes me, concern written all over his face. Same as earlier today. I don't think I've ever had *anyone* worry about me this much in my entire life the way he has in the last day.

"You're welcome to sleep if you want," he says. "I've got a few more things to take care of. I told Rhett to call me when he's done at the motel."

I smile weakly. "I thought I was your tag-along." I admit, it's been fun riding around with him. Probably the most fun I've had in months.

His dark eyes linger on mine. "Get some rest, Maci. I'll be right here."

My breath hitches. Why was that...exactly what I needed to hear? "Okay."

<center>~~~</center>

The high-pitched ding of a door opening rouses me from a heavy sleep. Slowly peeling my eyes open, the fog clears to Duke getting into the driver's seat, his phone pressed to his ear.

"Thanks, Rhett. I appreciate it," he says quietly. "No...I don't know, man. I don't want to talk about it. Yeah, so who told you to try? I figured as much." He sighs heavily. "I don't need everyone tiptoeing around the subject. I was caught off guard last Sunday, that's it, all right? I don't know how many times I have to say that. No, I haven't been ignoring anyone. Jesus Christ, man, you're worse than Ma."

He finally glances over at me, noticing I'm awake. A slow, handsome smile spreads across his face. "Listen, I've gotta go. I'll see you soon." He hangs up as I sit up with a stretch. "Sorry 'bout that. Didn't mean to wake you."

I roll my neck, feeling the unfortunate late afternoon nausea setting in. "You didn't. How long was I out?" I ask, reaching for my phone on top of my purse.

"About an hour," he grunts. "Did you want to get a bite to eat before I take you back to your room? Rhett said it was heating up quick, but I'd like to give it a bit longer to warm the place up."

I rub my temple. "Um, yeah, nothing too heavy though. I'm a little nauseous."

He nods, taking the truck out of park, and leaving the gas station he stopped at. "I'll drive down main, and if you see anything that looks good, say the word."

I smile, secretly loving how doting he's being. But I already know what I want, and he's not going to like what I have in mind...

⸺ℓℓℓ ⸺

"Maci," Duke bites out, following me out of the grocery store with my single jar of peanut butter in hand. "You need to eat something. This isn't a meal."

"It is when you're pregnant," I sing-song, carrying my prize across the parking lot.

He scowls, helping me into the passenger seat. "You need a real meal. Not fuckin' fruit, chips, and peanut butter. You're not a vegetarian, are you?"

I roll my eyes. So dramatic. "No, Duke, I'm not a vegetarian. I eat meat. I just want some peanut butter. The *baby* wants peanut butter. And I'm not going to deny my baby what it wants."

His eyes narrow. "You're so full of shit. The baby doesn't want peanut butter, you do."

I giggle. "Okay, we both do. But still. I am craving it, so it counts."

I can tell he's trying hard to be annoyed at this, but the twitch at the corner of his lip screams otherwise. Closing my door, he jogs around to the driver's side and jumps in. "All right, well, what else is *the baby* craving then?"

I scrunch my nose. "You're not going to like the answer..." I trail off at the sound of his irritated huff. "You can't be mad at me. I've been getting a little late afternoon morning sickness the last few days. It's hard for me to eat anything when I'm nauseous," I admit. "I'll order something later for dinner."

Duke lets out a long, aggravated sigh as we head to the motel. He's eerily quiet on the way—quieter than he's been all day. He can't really be mad about the peanut butter, can he?

"Do you have any plans tonight?"

"You mean *besides* texting you a picture later as proof of me ordering myself dinner?" I say, trying to lighten the strange air between us that's come out of nowhere.

He chuckles deeply. *Mission accomplished.* "After that."

I shrug. He knows I don't know anyone in this town—in all of Montana—and I've been riding around with him all day.

"I'd invite you to dinner, but it's for my brother's fiancée's birthday," he starts. "But, uh, after, there's a band playing at Tavern Nine. It's a local bar. Anyway, yeah, the party—if that's what you'd call it—is moving there afterward. Didn't know if that'd be something you'd be interested in or not."

I raise a brow. "What time?"

"Band usually starts around eight," he says, turning into the motel parking lot. "It's country night, so it'll probably be pretty packed."

I nod, biting my lip and wondering if this is a friendly invite or a weird, Montana way of asking me out. Do I want him to ask me out? *You're pregnant with someone else's baby, why would he?* I've quite literally got baggage growing inside of me.

And now I've hurt my own feelings.

He parks the truck. "Anyway, if you're interested, let me know beforehand and I can swing by to pick you up."

"Okay," I say as he gets out and comes around to my side.

When we step into the motel room we're greeted with a warm gust of air and a solid working heater. Duke stays close to the door so as not to track snow in the room. I feel his eyes on me as I kick off my boots and set my purse and jar of peanut butter onto the table.

"Thanks for tagging along with me today," he says.

I laugh, facing him. "You didn't give me much of a choice." I smile. "But thanks for letting me come with you. It was fun."

He watches me for a long moment, studying me in a way I get the sense he's...looking for something. He clears his throat. "All right, well, I better get going. If you need anything—"

"Let you know. Yes, I remember."

He grins wide, dark eyes alight with humor. "I'll talk to you later," he says, leaving with a close of the door behind him.

I plop onto the bed, a bundle of nerves and butterflies.

What am I doing?

I can't be doing...whatever the heck this feeling is. I need to focus. I'm only here because my car broke down on my way to a new job and a new life. I need to regroup and work out my next move.

Besides, a guy like Duke doesn't want a damaged, needy, pregnant woman up his ass. I can be his friend, though, like he said. Because *that*, I do need. One person I can turn to when I need to vent, or...bounce life-changing decisions off of other than a growing bump.

Gosh, I sound depressing.

Don't you mean lonely?

It's nearing six when I finally place an order for a grilled chicken wrap and fries from a local pizzeria. That's when I start to weigh my options. And the more I do, I realize I might only have one. Because when I tried to search for a transmission to fit my car...I came up short. Flipping through sites using words like 'backorder' and 'out of stock.'

A ding from my phone brings me back from a near mental breakdown.

Duke: *You were right.*

I smile at the message as the next one comes through.

Duke: *My mom is chewing me out tenfold for ignoring her earlier.*

Me: *I hate to say I told you so, but...*

Duke: *Very funny.*

Duke: *I'm still waiting on my picture of your dinner.*

Me: *It should be here any minute. I ordered from some place called Perry's.*

Duke: *They're pretty good. What'd you get?*

There's a knock at my door a second later. I pay the delivery guy, tip him, and take my food with gusto, not realizing how hungry I was until I smell the mouthwatering aroma of fresh food. I set the containers on the table and snap a quick picture. I send it to Duke as I sit down to eat.

Duke: *Looks good. How was your peanut butter?*

Me: *We loved it. I even ditched the spoon and used a few chips as scoops.*

Duke: *That actually sounds pretty good.*

Me: *How's the birthday dinner going?*

Duke: *Fine.*

Me: *Sounds riveting.*

Duke: *Just more bullshit.*

I fight the urge to ask him to elaborate when a thought comes to mind...

Me: *How much do you think I could get if I decided to sell my car?*

Duke: *Not much with the problems it has unless you plan on trading it in. Why? You thinking about ditching it?*

Me: *Maybe. Just trying to weigh out my options.*

Duke: *That might be your best bet.*

Duke: *Like I said before, I'll do my best to get you up and running, but there's gonna be a wait.*

Truthfully, I didn't believe him before. Now, after a few Google searches later, my unlucky streak has yet to break.

Duke: *So, you thinking of buying a new car then?*

Me: *Sorry to bother you with this. You probably want to be focusing on dinner with your family rather than texting me about car stuff.*

Duke: *I'd rather be texting you about anything than be a part of whatever conversations are going on around me.*

Me: *I don't want to be the reason you get in trouble again.*

Duke: *She is kind of glaring at me...*

Me: *Better put the phone down before you don't have any thumbs.*

Duke: *Fine, but if I send an S.O.S. in the next hour, I expect you to call me acting like something horrible has happened and you need me to come to your aid straight away.*

Me: *That bad?*

Duke: *Yes. Can I count on you?*

Me: *Always.*

⁓⁓⁓

I eat half my dinner before I decide to take a hot shower. I keep my hair tied up in case I decide to go to this 'Tavern Nine' Duke invited me to.

When I looked it up online earlier, it seemed like a popular spot. A lot of five-star reviews mentioning this 'Saturday band night.' Everyone in the pictures appear like they're hunting for a date—all done up and dancing.

He did say it was country night, and I do have something I *could* wear that wouldn't look horrible. But a pregnant chick going to a crowded bar only to drink non-alcoholic beverages and start yawning by nine? I don't know...

Granted I'm not necessarily showing quite yet, and I know over the next few weeks, I'll start to show. This might be my last chance to go out without getting strange looks.

Crap. It's after 8:00 PM though, and I haven't heard anything from Duke after our text conversation. The bar isn't too far—walking distance, in fact. I could make it there in fifteen or twenty minutes. I peek out the curtains. It's a clear December night, no wind, and just under freezing. A stark contrast to last night's storm.

"Screw it," I whisper, glancing down to my belly. "Let's go party hardy, baby."

Duke

I STARE AT MY phone for probably the hundredth time since I've sat down at this damn high-top bar table. I thought she'd want to come out.

Was I reading her wrong all day?

I've been out of the game for so long...I probably did. It took me a year after Rachel died to take a woman out. I've had a few scattered hook-ups over the last few years, but nothing ever gets past that. I've never wanted it to. I've been holding myself back from more, I know it.

But now... Fuck. It's 8:37 PM and she's all I can think about. What is she doing? Did she like her chicken wrap? Did it make her sick? Is she already asleep? Maybe if I text her—

"Duke," Butch bites out, catching my attention. I look up to him glaring at me. "I asked you a question."

"What do you need?" I grunt.

He doesn't answer, choosing to scowl at me instead. *Asshole.*

"He asked who the hell some *Maci* chick is," Stan says on a burp, sitting beside me.

Goddammit, Levi. My gaze scans the two tables we have pushed together to seat all eight of us at the rear of the bar, and a packed dance floor at my back. Yet everyone seems to have their attention on me. Something I'd rather not have.

From where I'm sitting on the end, to my right is Butch and his fiancée, Cassidy. Next to her is her best friend, Alison, then her boyfriend Tanner on the other end—who works for Butch. To my left is Stan, Butch's best friend and head foreman for his logging company. Beside him is Levi and Rhett.

A few of Cassidy's friends she invited are scattered around the bar, coming to and from the table. One of them perched on Levi's lap. And I know she invited them for me.

I fucking know it. The second we got here, she gave me a look. Her words from earlier at the coffee shop coming back to me. *I didn't know you were dating.* She thinks she's slick, but I see right through her and my family.

They're worried about me. And I hate that more than anything.

Saturday band nights are a regular thing for us, and I'm sure Cassidy is trying to get in as much time here with Butch before they're spending Saturday nights at home—planning a wedding, a baby, a future. The same three topics of conversation I've been forced to sit through all evening.

"She's a customer," I force out, hating the sound of it even as I say it.

"You told me she was a friend," Levi chimes in with a smirk.

"Was that whose motel room you had me at this morning?" Rhett asks, and I glare at him.

"Why were you at the motel?" Butch asks Rhett.

Rhett jerks his chin at me. "Duke had a job for me. One of the rooms had a faulty heater. I went out and fixed it. He said it was for a friend."

These idiots are unreal. I might as well not even be here.

Butch turns his stern expression to me. "What the fuck is the deal, Duke? I don't hear from you all week. You blow me off for some dead car on the side of the road. Now you're callin' Rhett for help instead of me?"

Here we go again...

Cassidy leans into Butch's side, and he drops his arm from the back of her chair to around her waist. "Babe, relax," she whispers as my brother's jaw ticks.

He shakes his head, taking an angry swig of his beer.

"It's not personal," I say. "I've been busy. Shop's been busy. Shit is coming together with the house. That's it." I chug a third of my beer so I don't have to say anything else on the subject.

"So how is the house coming?" Cassidy asks with a faint smile, attempting to redirect the subject—and her fiancé. "I'd love to see the progress you've made."

"You should've gone earlier, Cass," Levi announces, his eyes alight with mischief. The damn troublemaker he is. Ever since we were kids, he can't help ratting on one of us to watch the shit unfold. "Duke was giving tours."

Cassidy's brow furrows, but Butch beats her to the punch. "Who the fuck to?"

I open my mouth to respond when a light tap hits me on the shoulder and has me turning.

Maci's stunning smile fills my vision and it's like a whole room disappears until all I can see is her. *She came.*

Her deep red hair flows evenly down either side of her busty chest. She's done up to the nines—and I swear she's glowing—wearing high-waisted black leggings, a low-cut maroon long-sleeve that hugs tight to her mouthwatering hourglass curves, and battered brown cowgirl boots that look like they've seen mud.

"Hey." She smiles, lifting her hand in an awkward wave while holding her purse and flimsy coat in the other.

I push back on my stool to stand. "Hey, when did you get here?"

"Like five minutes ago," she says. "I've been looking for you. I thought finding your tall ass would've been a lot easier."

I grin. "You should've texted me. I would've stood up for you."
She giggles.

"You didn't walk here, did you?" I ask, my jaw tight at the thought. She scrunches her nose in the same cute as fuck way she did earlier over craving a jar of peanut butter. I'm a goner for that look.

Stan coughs loudly enough to catch my attention. I turn and all eyes are on us.

"Hey, Maci," Levi shouts. "Nice to see you again."

Maci smiles kindly. "You too, Levi."

I gesture to her at my side. "Everyone, this is Maci," I announce, quickly going through the motions to introduce her to everyone. The entire time, I keep an eye on Butch. He hasn't taken his eyes off her and how close she's drifted to me. And while I can't get enough, my brother has a look etched into his gaze that could kill.

I take Maci's coat and drape it over mine on the back of the chair then pull it out for her to sit. I lean down to whisper in her ear, "Did you want something to drink?"

She places a hand on my forearm, squeezing it as she whispers, "Yes, but don't leave me here alone. I think there's something wrong with your brother..."

I throw my head back with a laugh and take her hand in mine. I ignore everyone and walk her hand-in-hand over to the bar, ordering myself another beer and a virgin raspberry mojito for her.

"I would've picked you up," I tell her, paying for the drinks.

She rolls her eyes. "I knew you were going to say that. I decided last minute. It was after eight by the time I started to get ready."

"Still," I grunt. "You said you'd call."

Her smile drops into a yelp as she's roughly bumped from behind by a couple of rowdy assholes. She's pushed forward and nearly straight into the bar top. I wrap an arm around her and draw her into me, shoving back the guy who bumped her.

"Watch it," I growl. He puts his hands up, giving a weak apology to Maci before he retreats. Maci sags against me for a moment and my chest tightens. "You all right?"

She nods, righting herself. "Yeah."

We take our drinks and weave our way through the growing crowd. I keep a firm hold on Maci's hand as we do. The *need* to keep her close is uncontrollable. I *have* to. It's like there's an outside force demanding it of me. And I listen.

When we return to the table, Levi is yanked onto the dance floor by one of Cassidy's friends, whom I never caught the name of. The timing is perfect, however. "Move down, Stan," I say.

Maci takes his spot and I return to mine beside her. Butch's over assessing expression hasn't faltered and it resumes the moment we're comfortable. I kick his shin under the table, and his head snaps to me. "Knock it off," I growl lowly.

Stan stands with a clap of his hands. "All right, fuckers, are we doing birthday shots or what?" He points around the table before landing on Maci, he asks, "What's your poison, pretty lady?"

I clench my jaw with a tick at his choice of words.

Butch snorts, eyeing me as he toys with the neck of his beer bottle between his fingers. Watching me, her—us. And I don't like what he thinks he sees.

"I'm all set, thank you," Maci says, sipping her drink.

Stan groans dramatically. "Aw, come on. We're already down one here tonight cause she's pregnant. Don't tell me you are, too."

Maci covers her mouth, nearly spitting out her drink. I quickly hand her a napkin from the dispenser on the table. She takes it with a cough. "Thank you."

Cassidy laughs, waving Stan away. "Don't mind him, he's an ass," she says to her. "You're welcome to take my birthday shots, though. They're free all night."

"You're pregnant?" Maci asks in surprise.

Cassidy nods with a bright smile. "Yeah, seven weeks tomorrow."

Maci looks at me with wide eyes, and I wish more than ever I could read her mind at this very moment. "Oh," she breathes. "Congratulations."

Stan huffs. "Sooo, is that a yes or no to the shots? You know what, fuck it, I'll get 'em anyway. Someone will drink that shit." He leaves for the bar.

Cassidy leans over the table, pointing to Maci's drink. "I am curious. What are you drinking? It looks amazing."

"Oh, it's a raspberry mojito. Did you want to try it?"

Cassidy shakes her head. "I can't, but thank you."

"No, no. It's, um, a virgin. No alcohol," she tells her.

"You got a drinkin' problem?" Butch questions out of fucking *nowhere*. Of course, that'd be his first question on top of making her uncomfortable with his damn leering.

"Really, man?" I bite out. "Does she look like she's got a drinkin' problem?"

Maci bites her lip nervously. Her gaze darts around the table as a flush comes over her chest and neck.

"You don't need to answer that," I tell her, glaring at my brother.

"No, I—well, I wasn't going to say anything." She sighs. "But, yeah, I'm...pregnant. That's why I'm not drinking."

Every head at the table snaps to me with eyes as wide as saucers.

Idiots. The whole lot of them. It was a mistake coming out tonight. I should've faked stomach pain and left an hour ago. I'm too irritated as it is for this shit.

"No, it's not—" Maci waves her hands frantically. "I'm not from here. My car broke down on the side of the road last night, and Duke stopped to help me. I'm staying at Whitetail Motel while I'm stuck here," she rapid fires, feigning a pained smile. "Happy Birthday, by the way."

"Wait. You're stuck here?" Alison chimes in. "Where are you from?"

"Oklahoma. And yeah, sort of. At least until I decide what I want to do."

"Where's the father?" Butch asks bluntly. My hands fist in plain sight on the table. If he wasn't about to be a father himself, I'd kill him.

Cassidy swats him on the arm. "Will you stop," she scolds, turning her attention to a flustered Maci. "How far along are you?"

"Ten weeks, four days," she replies.

"Where were you going before you got here?" Alison asks curiously with a giddy-for-the-gossip expression I've seen far too many times. I hate it.

I hate it so much I jerk my chair back to stand and get Maci the hell out of here when Stan returns with a tray full of shots. "Shots, motherfuckers. Drink up."

The tension strung tight in my chest doesn't ebb until Maci reaches for me. She gives me a faint smile, her hand resting on my thigh once I retake my seat beside her. I lean in to whisper in her ear, "Say the word, and we'll go."

Everyone takes a shot—except for Cassidy and Maci, of course. We raise the shots and shout a booming *Happy Birthday* to Cass. The night takes off from there, and I fight hard to ignore my brother and his talent of getting under my skin these last few weeks. Cassidy's sole attention seems to be on Maci, though, and Butch clearly has nothing better to do but eavesdrop on their conversation.

Out of the corner of my eye, I spot a man spinning some girl around and around and around until she's far too close to where Maci's sitting. I grab her, but I'm not fast enough. Maci gasps when the woman collides with her back and jolts her forward. I pull her to me—yet again—before she can hit the table. The chick apologizes up and down to Maci, then goes right back to dancing.

"Jesus." Maci blows out an exaggerated breath, looking up at me with my arms wrapped around her. "I thought you said it was country night, not bumper cars."

I should've known a packed bar wasn't the safest place for her. But hell if all I wanted was an excuse to see her. Keeping her here feels selfish now... Yet I can't seem to find it in me to force her to leave with me until she's ready.

"Butch," I grunt. "Switch seats with Maci."

For once, my brother doesn't give me shit. He stands, swapping spots so the precious cargo is tucked away from the rowdy crowd against the far wall.

We settle back in and watch the band for a while. Well, everyone else does, because all I'm watching is *her*. Cass finally decides to taste Maci's non-alcoholic drink, and the face she makes when she does has Butch standing right away. "What the hell is it called?"

Maci smiles. "Virgin raspberry mojito."

"Get two," his fiancée beams, blowing him a kiss.

Butch glances at me. "Watch them."

I nod. He doesn't even need to tell me, I haven't stopped.

"How long have you two been together?" Maci asks Cassidy.

"Together for seven months, engaged for almost two," Cassidy says. "Sorry, he was asking you all those questions. He tends to get a little...protective of his family."

I scoff loudly, taking a swig of my beer. That's a damn understatement.

"I don't blame him. I mean, I *am* an outsider crashing your birthday."

"My birthday isn't until Wednesday. We're just celebrating early," Cassidy adds. "Besides, I'm happy for the fellow pregnant sober buddy in this sea of drunk people."

Maci laughs. "I was worried about the same thing. But I figured I better go while I still feel like it. I was already in my pjs about to pick a movie when I talked myself into it."

"Oh, that sounds so good right now," Cassidy whines. "I swear, I've never been more tired in my life than these last few weeks. If you don't mind me asking, how's your pregnancy been so far? I need someone else to compare mine to. None of my friends are pregnant or have kids."

Despite myself, I strain my ears to listen over the loud surroundings. No better than my brother, it seems. I snort.

"Pretty good. I get some regular morning sickness and late afternoon nausea, but nothing crazy. The exhaustion is a given, though. I heard it gets better in the second trimester."

Cassidy leans in. "Sorry to be so blunt, but I have to ask... Are you like *insanely* horny all the time?"

I choke on my beer. My throat burning as I cough profusely.

A gentle hand pats my back. "Are you okay?" Maci asks. Her voice. Her touch. That damn question. My cock throbs in my jeans at the very thought of her...*cravings* needing to be satisfied.

I cough, nodding. "Yeah, I'm good."

Butch returns with two virgin mojitos and a couple of beers for us. "You good, man?"

I chug down the remainder of my beer and take the new one with a rushed swig. The chilled liquid soothes my throat. *Fuck*. I feel like I might need a dozen more if I'm going to sit here and listen to Maci's sex life.

Cassidy stares at me, a smile playing on her lips that's giving me cause for concern. "Sorry, Maci, I didn't even ask. Are you single or taken?"

And there it is. It was only a matter of time.

Maci keeps her attention on me even as I glare at my soon-to-be sister-in-law. "Single," she replies blindly to Whitetail's new #1 shit stirrer. Levi better step up his game after tonight. "You sure you're okay?"

I grin, wiping my hand over my mouth with a chuckle. "Yeah, just went down the wrong pipe is all."

The conversation lightens up—*thankfully*. Although, my thickening cock doesn't miss the fact Maci never responds to Cass' previous question. And I would know, I was listening *diligently*.

"So, Maci, what do you do?" Stan burps out after another shot.

"I'm a yoga instructor and, funny enough, I taught line dancing on the weekends," she replies.

Yoga instructor? "No shit," I say as heat bubbles in my core.

"Well, shit." Stan pouts. "Where did you say you found her, Duke?"

I scoff, giving her thigh a squeeze under the table. "Sorry, man. There was only one on the shelf."

Maci laughs, laying a hand over mine.

"I need to see all my ladies out on the dance floor," the lead singer of the band booms through the microphone. "It's time to show these men how to make the earth quake."

Alison leaps from her seat, grabbing Cassidy by the arm. "Oh my god, yes. I love this song. Let's go."

Cassidy laughs, standing and turning to Maci. "Come on, Maci. Let's see what the yoga instructor from Oklahoma can do."

"I don't—"

"Preggos stick together," Cassidy snaps back. "And it's my birthday."

Maci sets her purse on the table. "Okay, fine."

Cassidy and Alison scurry to the dance floor. I chuckle as Maci huffs. "Laugh it up, bossy mechanic," she says. "You're next." She winks, sauntering around me to the dance floor with a slide of her hand over my shoulders. It sends a thrill of desire through me—the kind you get when you want someone...more than you should.

Butch shifts his chair beside me to watch them get in line with a dozen other women as the song picks up tempo. "You got a thing for her?" It's a clear question. One he already knows the answer to.

And one I'm not sure I'm ready to admit to myself yet.

She'll be back on the road toward Alaska before I know it.

I swig my beer and ignore him—and myself. Choosing to enjoy the night while it's dancing right in front of me.

It isn't long before everyone on the dance floor is following Maci's lead. Cassidy and Alison watch her every move, copying her the best they can. I don't know how they do things down in Oklahoma, but...damn.

She's clapping, stomping her feet, kicking, shimmying, jumping in her sexy-as-fuck boots. She spins around and her shirt rides up, exposing the flawless skin of her waist. A wide-spread smile crosses her face as she mouths the words to the song. I'm grinning from ear to ear, loving how happy she looks right now. When she does a turn, her beautiful hair flips as she catches my eye. She sends me a slick wink, pops her hip, and smacks her ass my way, sending a jolt straight to my cock.

Fuckin' hell.

Stan whistles lowly. "Butch, I quit. I'll be scoping the streets for chicks stranded on the side of the road. Duke, man, you hiring?"

They share a hearty laugh, but all I can do is grin, never taking my eyes off her.

Nine.

Maci

When the song ends, everyone claps. "Now grab yourself a partner, ladies, and drag 'em out here," the singer announces as the band starts up another country twang.

Alison sprints to grab Tanner who goes without question. While Cassidy takes Butch's hand. He pretends to fight it like he doesn't want to go, but anyone can see he does. It's sweet how in love they all are.

Duke and his brother Butch look a lot alike, but I see the differences in personality and how they carry themselves. Cassidy is about my height, maybe a few inches taller. Brown hair and stunning deep blue eyes, it's no question she drew her fiancé in with a bat of her eye.

They pass me by as I go to Duke.

"You're pretty good," he says.

I take the seat beside him to catch my breath. "Do you dance?"

He shrugs. "Yeah. I mean, I can. Not as good as you, that's for sure."

I nudge him playfully with my elbow. "I'm sure you do all right."

He keeps his gaze on me as he swigs his beer back and slams it on the table. He stands with his hand out with a lopsided grin.

Does he have any idea what he's doing to me when he looks at me like this? Like I'm the only woman in the room.

As if I wasn't already riled up seeing him in those snug jeans and cowboy boots. He had to put on a charcoal grey T-shirt a size too small stretched tight over his broad chest and thick biceps while showing off a tattoo I didn't know he had on his left forearm.

I bite my lip with a smile, slapping my hand in his. He chuckles. I slide off the high stool and Duke leads us out onto the dance floor. It's a more upbeat country song. A lot of swaying, spinning, real dancing—not just bumping and grinding.

I giggle as he twirls me around, then brings me in tight against his solid frame. With a firm hand on my lower back, he holds my hand with the other, my free hand resting on his bicep. Our eyes stay locked as we dance. And I have to admit, he's pretty good.

His hand trails to my hip, a bit more pressure behind his grip as he holds me close. My breath hitches. I want to kiss that smug look right off his face. Because he knows *exactly* what he's doing to me.

The song ends, changing to a slower ballad with more of a grind to it. No doubt to keep the couples on the dance floor. When

I move to step away, Duke swiftly spins me into a dip before spinning me against his chest. I laugh, throwing my arms up and around his thick neck. "Smooth."

He chuckles. "I try."

We dance slower, grinding, and swaying. And it's...nice. Being this close to him. Being able to smell his cologne on my clothes. Feel his touch on my skin. When he dips his head into the crook of my neck I nearly melt. *Yes.*

Maybe I *could* let my car breaking down decide where I call home...

They call it fate, right?

Everyone finds their way to the table a few songs later. Jokes and stories are thrown about freely. Laughter and cheers float around me. Duke's arm is across the back of my chair, keeping me close to his side, and making it impossible for me to wipe the smile off my face.

When I cover my mouth to a yawn, he rubs my arm. "Ready to go?"

I nod, not bothering to say I can walk myself to the motel. I know he won't let me, especially this late. I don't think I've stayed up past eleven in... Well, a long while, we'll just say that.

Duke stands with me, helping me with my coat.

Cassidy slides off Butch's lap. "Oh, thank god. I didn't want to be the first one to leave."

"Babe, we could've gone whenever you wanted," Butch says, rising to get their things.

She rolls her eyes. "Yeah, well, I didn't want to be *that* pregnant."

"Hey," I say, and she laughs. "Well, not to sound even *more* pregnant," I tease. "Could you show me where the bathroom is?"

Duke wraps an arm around my waist, catching my attention. "We'll be waiting outside."

"Okay." I sigh as butterflies take flight at the way he's gazing down at me.

Should I? I mean, could we...

Cassidy waves me to follow her lead as we head for the ladies' room. I use the stall first. "Sooo, what do you think of Duke?" she asks through the door.

"What do you mean?"

"Um, hello," she says in a *duh* tone. "He's all over you. And the way y'all were dancing... I mean, come on. I don't know if you're looking for anything, unless you are..." she trails off, waiting for me to fill in the blank.

"I'm not looking for anything," I say, and even to my ears, it sounds like a lie. Evan wasn't the best boyfriend—he had a whole other life, after all. I've never been with a guy like Duke before. He's...great. Knowing my luck, I'd ruin it and end up hurting us both. "I'm only here temporarily."

Cassidy huffs, going into the stall when I exit to wash my hands. "What, um, about the baby's father?"

"He's not in the picture." The simple, true-ish, straight-to-the-point answer saddens my mood. *When Duke asks you, are you going to feed him another half-truth, too?* My stomach plummets.

What would he think of me if he knew the truth?

Homewrecker, the word echoes in my mind in the same tone my father shouted at me the last time I saw my parents.

Cassidy comes out of the stall, catching my eye in the mirror. "I'm sorry."

I shrug. "It's for the best."

She washes her hands. "Well, I don't know how long you're here for, but I'd love to hang out sometime. It's hard trying to talk to Butch about how I'm feeling. He tries to understand, but it's not the same as someone who's going through it, too, ya know?"

"Oh, I know." *Boy, do I know...*

We walk through the dying crowd at the bar to reach the front door. We step outside expecting the boys to be there waiting, but only a huddle of smokers lean against the building. "They might be pulling the trucks around," Cassidy says, tapping on her phone while we wait off to the side.

Arms wrap around me from behind, and I smile. Sneaky man. I turn in his arms. "Where did you—" The words die in my throat when the face of a stranger fills my vision. It takes me a split second to realize it's *his* hands that are on me—not Duke's. I take a step back, and he reaches for me. "Hey, beautiful," he moans, blowing cigarette smoke in my face.

I cough, waving at the smoke and swatting his hands away.

"Aw, come on. Don't be like that." He chuckles darkly.

Gross. I scoff, turning to walk away only for a loose smack to hit my ass. I gasp, whirling around. He grabs me.

"Hands off, Colt," Cassidy yells, shoving at the stranger's slimy paws locked on my jacket.

My heart pounds as he yanks me around like a rag doll.

"Fuck off, Cass," he barks. His arm releases me for a moment to push her away, when his wrist is caught by a large, heavy hand. Butch stands tall and as intimidating as ever, forcing his way between the man and me.

Another pair of hands tugs at me. I jump, spinning on my heel and stumbling into his strong, sturdy embrace. Duke. *Thank god.*

His gaze is dark and...not on me. "He's mine, Butch," he growls. *Wait, what?*

Cassidy takes my hand, ushering me with her to stand beside Butch.

"What are—"

I don't get to ask what's going on before Duke throws a *sickening* punch to the man's jaw. The echo of bones cracking has me feeling ill.

I gape as Duke moves with ruthless precision. Landing three hard hits to the drunk man's face, a nauseating hit to the gut, and a dead weight toss into the snowbank—peppered with stones and dirty cigarette butts.

I take several steps back. Who is this guy? Surely not the sweet, over-caring man I rode around with all day.

"Maci," Cassidy calls out to me. "Don't worry, it's okay."

I shake my head in disbelief. In what way is Duke pummeling this guy okay? I hurry toward the sidewalk, hugging myself as I backtrack to the motel. *I should've just picked a damn movie.*

"Maci!" The misplaced panic in his voice almost stops me in my tracks—*almost.* I pick up the pace instead. And it's not another minute before the rumble of Duke's truck trails along the road beside me. "Maci, get in the truck."

I keep walking even as I glance at him. "Are you insane?"

He snarls—legitimately *snarls*—and hits the gas. The truck whips ahead to block my path at the next intersection I need to cross. Unbelievable.

"Get in."

"No," I say calmly. I start to climb over the large snowbank to get around him.

"Maci," he shouts so loud it startles me. I slip on a frozen chunk of snow and lose my footing, falling flat on my ass. I suck in a sharp breath. *Oh, that's cold.*

"Shit," he bites out. The dinging of his truck door is loud in the cool, silent night.

I sigh, lying in the snow. I look up at the clear night sky filled with bright, beautiful stars. *Wow.*

Duke's face fills my line of sight, towering over me with a worry-etched expression. "Are you okay?"

"You're blocking the view," I say.

"What?"

I point to the sky. "They're so much brighter here." I suppose light pollution from the city I lived in had something to do with that, but still, it's hard to look away.

He tips his head up, and the second he does, I bring my leg up and kick out his knee. He lands in the snow beside me with a grunt. "Shit. That's cold," he hisses.

I burst into laughter.

He looks less than amused as he extends his hand. "Come on, you're going to freeze."

I take his hand with both of mine and yank him to lie down beside me. He braces his arm in the snow, his face hovering inches from mine as he chuckles, "You're out of your mind."

"Me?" I snort. "You're the psycho who just beat a guy for no reason."

His smile quickly fades. "He had his hands on you, Maci. Trust me, he deserved it," he says, still visibly angered even as he brushes my hair from my face. "I'm sorry you had to see that," he adds softly, "but I won't apologize for keeping you safe."

Something akin to fear crosses his face as he searches mine. Despite the chill, my body ignites in a way that has me questioning my resolve. It's not the first time he's used that word. Safe. Is that what he thinks? He's been keeping me safe these last few days? I don't need to think much more on it, I'm sure the jury would agree—he most assuredly has.

"Where were you?" I whisper.

"Oh, uh..." His gaze darts to the side. "Taking a leak."

My nose scrunches. "Outside?" I accuse. "With your brother?"

He shrugs. "Maybe."

We burst into a fit of laughter that only dies down when I start to shiver. "Let's get you inside," he says, and I nod. Snaking my arms around his strong neck, he lifts me from the side of the snowbank and onto the sidewalk. I brush off my backside while he pats my damp coat, then helps me into the passenger seat.

I watch him climb back over the snowbank. When he slips, having to grab onto his plow to stay upright, his gaze snaps to me through the windshield. I'm in tears laughing, watching him hold on and chuckle at himself.

He makes it over and gets in the truck. "For a second, I thought you were being a bit dramatic falling in the snow like that," he says, grinning, "but it's slick as shit over there."

I fan my eyes to dry the tears. "I am *not* dramatic." I laugh. "I fall gracefully."

He chuckles, driving us toward the motel. "I don't know if I'd call that graceful," he adds, grinning from ear to ear. He stops out front of my motel room door and throws the truck in park. His smile drops a little. "I didn't mean to scare you."

I pain a smile. "It was just a little...unexpected."

He sighs heavily. "I get that."

"But I trust you." The words spill from my lips before I can think better of it. I surprise myself with the truth of them. Do I? I suppose I do.

Duke rubs his face roughly. "Good. 'Cause I'm feeling like a real asshole over here. And that job is usually reserved for my brother."

"I bet." I smile, reaching for the door handle. "Thank you for inviting me out tonight, I had fun."

His dark eyes dip to my lips and linger there for a long moment before they meet mine once more. "Me, too."

I hesitate. My mind ricochets between what I want and what I shouldn't. I force my body to move, choosing to slide out of the truck. I hold onto the door while I debate inviting him in. Would he want to? I don't want this night to end, but I don't want to ruin it either.

"I'll see you later?" I say, a question more than anything else. And I hate how desperate I sound.

"Call if you need anything."

"If I had a dollar for every time you've told me that," I tease.

The sexy, crooked grin he sends my way has me realizing I *do* need something.

I have a craving—and it's him.

"Goodnight, Duke."

Ten.

Duke

I STARE AHEAD AS Maci pushes inside her motel room and closes the door behind her. My headlights beam at her window. The curtains are closed, but I still catch the flick of her turning on a bedside lamp.

"Just drive away, man. Drive away," I say to myself, tapping the steering wheel with my thumb. My leg jumping. Mind racing. *Fuck.*

I can still feel her hand in mine, her body pressed against me, my arms wrapped around her. I can still see her smile, hear her laugh, smell her perfume. She's so goddamn beautiful. So perfect. I haven't felt this way since...

I can't go there. I won't put her in that place.

She's not *her*. She'll never be *her*.

Maci's something else—something here and now. *Can I have it again?* I've spent one day with her. That's it. And here I am fiending like a lovesick puppy.

But I am.

I'm so fucking lovesick, craved, deprived—it *hurts.*

My phone dings with a text and I fish it from my back pocket.

Maci: *No strings attached.*

Blood rushes north and south as my heart hammers in my chest. *No strings,* she says. If she's learned anything at all about me in the last day, it's that I'm not good about detaching myself. Not when it comes to her, anyway.

I kill the engine and my palms feel heavy as I push open the truck door. I get out and stride to her door. When I knock, she calls out, "Who is it?"

I grin. "Your bossy mechanic."

She giggles from the other side of the door followed by the slide of the deadbolt. The door opens and my mouth goes dry. Her boots and coat are off and there's a play of a sexy smirk on her full lips. "Bummer, I was hoping for the milkman."

A growl escapes my throat as I swoop down and pick her up by her ass. She squeaks, wrapping her legs around my waist. Her arms lock around my neck and I kick the door shut behind me.

The second I do; she crashes her lips on mine with an intensity I've never felt before.

I grip her ass tighter and she moans into my mouth with a slight opening of her lips—tasting, begging for more. Our tongues glide over one another like we've kissed a hundred times. It's greedy and passionate. She's kissing me like I'm the only thing that matters. And I feel it deep, *deep* down—past the pain, the hurt, the past.

I need this. I need this *with her*.

If this is what it's like just to kiss her...

Carrying her to the bed, I lay her down and kick off my boots without breaking the kiss. Maci shifts, pushing my jacket off my shoulders with a nip to my lower lip. I tug it off and toss it to the side as she rips my hat off and flings it across the room. I grin against her lips.

Greedy girl.

Her nails scrape the back of my neck to twine her fingers through the short hair on the back of my head. I groan, pressing my weight onto her—gently. I hold myself up with one arm and trail the other down the curve of her body. Memorizing every inch. Thighs, ass, hips, the dip of her waist, the pop of her pillowy breasts.

"You're so fucking beautiful." I kiss her hard. Possessive. "In this room, you're *mine*. Do you understand?" I pant, needing this to feel real—with her, only her.

She looks up at me, her thumb caressing my bottom lip. Big, emerald eyes study me until she quietly agrees, "Yes."

"Fuck, doll face," I groan, roughly claiming her mouth. She moans when I bite her lip in return, then soothe it with a suck between my lips. Her body arches into me and her hands trail under my shirt to press against my skin. My cock strains painfully in my jeans—demanding that skin on skin contact.

I pull away to sit up between her thighs and take off my shirt.

"Oh, do I get a strip tease, too?" she teases.

I chuckle, bracing over her with a grind of my rock-hard cock against her pussy through her leggings. "You can have whatever you want, doll."

I'll give you the world if you let me.

Maci moans as I leave hot kisses down her jaw and neck. "Yes."

I start to move down her body, urging her to sit up. When she does, I help her out of her shirt and bra. Her breasts fall deliciously between us and I dip my head to suck one nipple into my mouth, kneading the other with my fingers.

She arches into my touch, her hands in my hair. With a wet pop, I release her stiff nipple to kiss her swollen lips. I tug at the waist of her leggings. Her breath hitches when I slide a hand inside to cup her pussy.

She's wet—slick with need. I trail my thick fingers through her folds.

"Duke," she gasps.

I rub her swelling clit. Her hips rise for more, and I push a finger into her hot, wet cunt. "Fuck," I hiss, curling my finger to rub against her channel. She twists, grinding down on my hand.

She's a moaning, writhing mess in my arms, and I can't get enough. I need *more.*

I pull my hand away, and she whimpers sweetly. Her gaze turns fiery as I bring my fingers, wet with her arousal, to my lips. I lick them and watch her watch me with avid eyes as I taste her. "So fuckin' good."

She reaches for my cock—but I need to feel her under my tongue first.

I urge her to lay back with a kiss as I grip the band of her pants and yank them down along with her panties. Leaving her naked before me.

I drop to my knees on the floor and drag her by her thighs, bringing her ass to the edge of the bed. I pause, taking in the sight of her glistening folds in the dim lighting. I rub her inner thighs and lay a tender kiss on her pussy. She shivers. "Your pussy is fucking perfect, baby," I say.

She lifts to her elbows, watching me with parted lips. "Duke..."

"Watch," I growl as I spread her and lick a long, firm press of my tongue through her slit. She squirms and moans and I grip her thighs to keep her spread for me. I flick my tongue along the sides of her clit, finding her spot until she's bucking against my face then suck at her gently.

Her legs begin to tremble and I look up. My cock pulses at her wrung taut. Flushed and needy. I push a finger into her core, doubling my efforts.

"Duke," she breathes as I pump my finger in and out of her, eating her sweet pussy. She falls back as her orgasm hits and she screams, coming hard. I watch her, feel her come on my tongue—and it's the hottest thing I've ever seen.

Coming down from her high, she goes to push me away from her sensitive flesh, but I hold firm. Trailing my tongue up and down her dripping pussy. "Goddamn," I growl, pumping my finger slowly, her juices drenching my hand.

Her legs tremble. "Duke."

I grin against her with a slow lick. "Yes, angel?"

Her laugh is breathy, sated. "Are you done?"

I rub the pad of my finger against her G-spot. "No, baby, I'm not done," I say, working her pussy again...and again. Her panting chants of my name urge me to make her come twice more before I finally stop. When I'm done with her, she's soaked the sheets as aftershocks have her trembling.

I lick my lips and massage her shaking thighs, wanting nothing more than to bury my cock deep inside her. She smiles breathlessly, sitting up on the edge of the bed. "Stand up."

I grin like a maniac and do as she says. I undo my belt and jeans, allowing my cock to spring free. Maci moans at the very sight of me, eager hands wrapping around my girth.

She looks up at me as she leans in, licking the damp head of my cock and stroking me torturously slow. I groan. This woman will be the death of me.

She sucks me into her hot, wet mouth. Hollowing out her cheeks as she forces me deep in her throat. I buck my hips, darting my hand out to fist her hair. "Fuck." If she keeps this up, I'm not going to last at all.

I jerk back. "Christ, beautiful." I grip her hair and force her head back to claim her lips with mine. "Get your sexy ass on that bed."

She laughs, crawling away only to give me a view of her perfect, heart-shaped ass. I kick off my jeans and boxers at lightning speed and crawl after her.

I grab her and flip her on her back. Her breasts bounce, chest heaving, panting as I prowl over her. She lifts her legs to wrap around my waist. "Tell me I can feel you," I groan, dipping to kiss her chest and neck as I settle in between her thighs.

My cock brushes the slick core of her pussy.

She moans, arching. "Wh—When was the last time you..."

I pause, gazing down at her. I search her eyes. *It's been close to a year since I've been with anyone like this*, I want to tell her. But I don't. Because what we're doing doesn't feel like anything I've ever had before...and I need her to know that.

"I'd never do anything to hurt you, Maci. I've got condoms in the truck, if you want me to get one, I will."

Her hands slide over my arms and around my neck to draw me in to kiss her.

"Are you sure?" I ask.

Maci lifts her hips in response, pressing the head of my cock into her a fraction. I grunt, holding steady even as my body hums to sink deep.

"Fuck me, Duke," she whispers against my lips—and I am far too weak to deny her.

I kiss her hard and reach between us, aligning my cock before thrusting into her. She sucks in a breath, her nails digging into my biceps. And I feel her. All of her. Wrapped around me. Wet, hot, tight. And she feels... So. Fucking. Good.

I grit my teeth, seated fully. She whimpers, hips twitching for more. I fall over her, needing to kiss her as I pump my cock slowly. Reveling in the sensation—the closeness—of her raw cunt snug around my unsheathed cock.

Maci digs her heels into my ass, lifting her hips and forcing me even deeper.

I groan, pulling out only to thrust into her with a snap of my hips. The bed and her legs shake as I slam into her.

If she wants me to *fuck her*, I'll fuck her.

I grip her hip, engulfing it in a sure hold as I tilt her pelvis and rub my cock against her G-spot. I fuck her like this until her pussy pulses around me. I take her leg and put it on my shoulder, pushing the other wide as I stare at our bodies connected.

I rub her swollen clit. "Harder," she cries.

Harder, deeper—I bite back my orgasm as her walls start to clench around me. "Come on my cock, baby," I grunt, slamming into her with a grind of my pelvis. Needing her to come. With me. For me.

Only me.

She screams my name once again as pleasure overcomes her, and I feel her come on my cock. I lean into her and pound her with a chase of my release. "Holy...fuck," I shout, coming hard with a shudder and her name on my lips.

Our panting breaths mirror as we come down. Maci cups my face in her hands, kissing me tenderly. Our tongues glide over one another. The kiss is slow, sensual—and my heart can't handle it.

I pump my cock, letting her milk every last drop from me.

"Still rather have the milkman?" I raise a brow, but I can't keep a straight face when she lights up with laughter. I grin and slide an arm under her. Falling beside her, I bring her to lay on top of me.

She lets out a quiet sigh, resting her head on my chest. I take the bunched-up comforter and throw it over us. She lifts her head to rest her chin on my chest. "Kiss me," she says, and I do. When I lay my head back down, she smiles. "The milkman, who?"

I chuckle, loving the glimmer in her eye. Gently brushing her hair out of her face, she rests her head on my chest. I hold her like that for some time, feeling her heart beat against mine—and I find myself falling. Hard. Far too fast to stop the path we're on. This was deeper than sex. We have a connection. And it's leaving me wanting more—more of *her*.

My chest tightens as her breathing evens out and I know it in my gut...

I've found it again.

And this time, I'm never letting go.

When I wake, I find Maci curled against my side. Her arm draped over my abdomen and a leg thrown over mine. She must've been still awake when I passed out because her hair is damp from a shower and she's washed off her makeup—looking even more beautiful without it. I lift the sheet, eyeing her clad in a navy blue tank, no bra, and white panties.

I check the bedside clock. 6:03 AM. My phone vibrates from somewhere on the floor and I slip my arm out from under her. Maci rolls onto her back with a breathy sigh, her tank bunched high on her waist—the picture of an angel.

I idly wonder if she caught me watching her sleep in my truck yesterday. I'd be lying if I said I didn't mindlessly drive around after I finished my errands solely not to wake her.

As I pull the covers over her, I pause, my gaze drifting to her stomach. Laying on her back slightly angled like this, I can see...her bump.

Without thinking, I lay a gentle hand over it. The mound is firmer than I thought it'd be. Sweet and small under my large, rough palm.

Hey, there...

Maci stirs and I yank my hand back. She rolls away from me to rest on her side and I use the movement to get up. I cover her once more, then tip-toe to the bathroom to clean myself from last night. My cock stirs when I realize I can still taste her on my lips.

I get dressed and check my phone to a few missed calls—no doubt work-related on a damn Sunday. I glance at the bed and watch her sleep for a long moment, torn with leaving when my phone rings for the third time.

I send her a text to let her know where I'll be and to message me when she wakes up. Her phone lights up on the nightstand. Satisfied, I tug my boots and coat on, then slip out the door to take my leave.

My *very* reluctant leave.

Eleven.

Maci

I ROLL OVER WITH a stretch, expecting to feel a hard chest beside me, but my hand hits cold, empty sheets. *Did he leave?* I strain to listen if he might be in the bathroom, but I don't hear any movement. Sighing, I reach for my phone.

It's just after nine, and I have an unopened text from three hours ago.

Duke: *Good morning, beautiful. I've got some work stuff to take care of this morning. Shoot me a text when you wake up. xo*

I smile, loving his cliché start to the message and the little 'xo' at the end. My joy, however, is cut short by a wave of nausea as I sit up. Ugh. *Good morning to you, too, little one.*

It's a slow start getting ready for the day—staying close to the bathroom in case morning sickness decides to take over two days in a row. I manage to put on a pair of jeans and a low-cut, white long-sleeve. I tug Duke's hoodie over my head for the third day in a row and flip my hair out around me. His strong, masculine scent wafts with the action, and I can't help the smile that comes to my lips remembering last night.

Last night was...passionate. I've never felt so connected to someone. So lost in them in the moment. The way that man kissed me... It was like nothing I've experienced. And how he held me after? I hum in bliss just recalling his warm, hard chest under me. The way his arms locked around me, keeping me in place.

I truly felt like he never wanted to let me go.

I wonder if he'd be interested in doing it again? I mean, I did say 'no strings attached.' I didn't say 'one time only.'

Deciding I need to get out of this stuffy motel room for some much-needed carbs for breakfast—on top of buckling down to plan out my next move—I tug on my boots.

Look for a car? A bus ticket to Alaska?

Or maybe...a job and apartment?

Here?

I stuff my laptop cord inside the pocket of Duke's hoodie and pull over my coat. I grab my purse, phone, and laptop, and head toward the coffee shop we went to yesterday, with a plan in mind.

It's a little colder today. The crunch of icy snow beneath my boots is loud, and the crisp December air fills my lungs. It's refreshing. Although, I can hear Duke now, complaining about me walking. I smile. The very thought of him sends heat to my *still-aching* core.

I arrive ten minutes later at the quaintest little brick coffee house at the center of town: Cup O' Joe. I open the door with a classic *chime* of a bell above me to announce my arrival.

"Maci," a vaguely familiar voice calls.

I lift my gaze to behind the counter. "Hey, Alison," I say, walking toward her. It's not as crowded as yesterday. A few tables full at the most. "You work here?"

"Oh, yeah, worked here for over two years now." She points over my shoulder. "So does Cassidy, but she's having a rough morning."

I thought I recognized her last night, but I've never been good with faces. I turn in her direction to find Cassidy wearing a matching apron and work shirt, sitting at the table by the window with her head in her hands. I know that look. Heck, I just experienced it.

Cassidy lifts her head. "Hey, Maci," she greets weakly.

"Nauseous?" I ask, and she nods. "Same. I'm here for carbs. Did you eat yet?"

She stands slowly, walking toward me. "I tried, but I got a whiff of the egg from the breakfast sandwiches and nearly vomited on a customer," she tells me, and I bite back a laugh at the visual. "I don't know if I have it in me today, Alison."

"I told you to go," Alison says. "I've got it covered here. We're slow this morning. Call Butch and have him come pick you up."

I stare at the rustic chalkboard menu on the wall behind her. "Do you have anything with peppermint in it?" I ask.

Alison points. "We've got peppermint tea, hot or cold. And a hot peppermint mocha, with or without coffee."

I smile and glance at Cassidy. "Peppermint helps with nausea," I tell her, and she perks up ever so slightly. "I'll take a peppermint mocha frappe. Extra whipped cream and two blueberry muffins."

"You got it, preggers," Alison laughs.

"I'll get the drink, Al," Cassidy says. "I'm making two. I need to try this. 'Cause if it works, Butch is buying stock in peppermint."

I pay, then take the seat by the window to settle in and pop open my laptop.

Cassidy arrives a few minutes later with my muffins and drink, setting it beside me. She plops down across from me with her matching, steaming mug held close. "How are you feeling this morning?" she asks, taking a tentative sip.

"Tired. Nauseous. Hungry," I say, blowing on the cup and watching the whipped cream melt for a moment before taking a small sip. "The usual."

She holds her mug with both hands. "Were you okay after last night? I wanted to call you, but Butch said Duke had it covered."

Oh, he had me covered, all right. "I was a little...caught off guard."

"Totally understandable," she says, "but don't let that cloud your judgment on Duke. He's an absolute sweetheart. Or Butch. He can be a bit intimidating meeting new people, and it didn't help he was in a mood last night. Duke and him have been…strained this last week. Butch isn't handling it well."

"Oh, I'm sorry."

Cassidy waves me off, smiling. "Don't be. You made last night *so* much better. Definitely lightened the tension between them."

I take a bite of my muffin; not wanting to be rude, but also too hungry to care.

"So, how long are you in town for?" she asks.

"Wait. You're traveling alone?" Alison adds, eagerly bouncing to the table to be a part of the conversation. "Where are you going?"

They stare at me with matching eager expressions. "Um, Alaska."

Alison whistles lowly. "That's a hell of a drive to be making by yourself. Oklahoma to Alaska? Sounds exhausting."

I snort. It is—or *was*?

"What's in Alaska?" Cassidy asks, leaning forward.

I try to wave them off with a shake of my head. "It's a long story. I don't want to bore you with it." Truthfully, I don't think I want them to know. Or anyone, for that matter. Well, maybe *one* person…

They whine in unison. "Please," Cassidy begs. "I've been dying over here for *hours*. I need the distraction. One pregnant lady to another."

It's the third time she's used that against me. I laugh and take another big bite of my muffin when my phone rings. It's Duke.

I hold a finger up to the nosey bodies watching me and swallow before answering, "Hey."

"Where are you?" he bites out.

My smile fades at his tone. "I came down to the coffee shop for breakfast. Why?"

"Fuck," he grunts. His voice fades and I hear him speak to someone. A loud, heavy slam of a door follows. "I told you to text me."

"Sorry, I got—"

"You scared the fuck out of me, Maci," he grits. "I'm at the motel now, been banging on the goddamn door worried something was wrong when you didn't answer. Christ. You could've at least texted me you were leaving the room."

"I—"

"And you walked," he growls in frustration. "Dammit, angel. It's below freezing out. There's ice on the sidewalks, you could've—"

"Duke," I snap. "Will you stop. I got sick this morning before I could reply to you. I was going to text you when I got here, but I got distracted."

I lift my gaze to Cassidy and Alison sharing a look, beaming at each other. My brow furrows at the strangeness of it. Then Alison swats her friend in the arm, pointing out the window.

We all stare as Duke whips into the parking lot. He throws the truck in park and glares at me through the windshield. He hangs up the phone, kicks open his truck door, and stalks through the front door without taking his eyes off me.

"Hey, Duke," Cassidy beams.

Alison stands. "Coffee? Two cream, one sugar, right?"

He doesn't respond, his dark eyes locked on me as he growls, "I told you to call me if you needed anything. You shouldn't be out walking in this cold, Maci."

Alison giggles, scurrying behind the counter. "Get him an extra-large," Cassidy sings, gesturing beside me. "Sit, Duke. Maci's only been here for like ten minutes. She's barely touched her muffins."

Duke rubs his face, sitting beside me. Visibly upset I didn't tell him where I was. What's the big deal? I'm a grown-ass woman. If I want to leave my motel room and walk down the street to get a damn muffin, I will.

Is this about last night?

"I'm sorry," I try again.

"It's fine. Just...text me next time, okay?" His voice is strained, and his gaze flies over me from head to toe as if to inspect me for damage. "You all right? You got sick this morning?"

I shrug. "Just a little nausea. I'm okay now."

"Oh, that reminds me," Cassidy chimes in, pulling out her phone. "I better text Butch and let him know I'm feeling better. Maci is a lifesaver, Duke. She told me about this peppermint thing that helps with nausea. The smell alone is helping."

Duke throws his arm around the back of my chair and abruptly yanks me to him until my side is pressed against him. "Glad to hear it, Cass."

Alison returns with Duke's coffee. "Did you want anything else?"

He hands her cash. "I'm set right now, Alison. Thanks."

She scurries away as a family of four strolls in the door dressed in heavy snow gear.

Duke lifts his chin to my laptop. "The Wi-Fi down at the motel?"

"No, um," I hesitate, then sigh. No point in hiding it, I suppose. "I was going to start working out a plan. You know, figure out what I want to do with my car and...everything else."

"Are you still going to Alaska?" Cassidy asks.

Duke's gaze stays on me even as a heated scowl morphs his features. He turns to aim it in her direction. I don't take long to study this odd change in his demeanor. He's clearly bothered by his future sister-in-law asking me this. But why?

"I'm not sure," I admit, watching for Duke's reaction out of the corner of my eye. "I've got a few options, or ideas rather. I'm just waiting to find out how much the repair on my car might cost me."

Duke sips his coffee. "I'll have a quote ready for you first thing tomorrow morning."

"What are your options?" Cassidy asks curiously.

I take in a deep breath. "Well, I've worked out a few... I can stay just long enough to fix my car, then hit the road. Or I can trade my car in and get something else, then go—and that's assuming I still have a job waiting for me when I get there. Or...I ditch my original plan for a new one and go with fate deciding this is home."

Cassidy gasps, her hands flying out around her. "Fate all the way." She smiles brightly, glancing between Duke and me.

Duke snaps his head to me, brow furrowed, jaw tight. But his eyes are soft, filled with emotion. His strong neck works as he swallows thickly. "You...think you might stay?"

My eyes never leave his even as my heart begins to pick up a rapid beat. "I might. I mean, it'd all depend if I could find a job and apartment here."

"Where were you going to live in Alaska?" Cassidy presses further.

"Extended stay motel until I signed the lease on an apartment."

Alison scurries back to the table, plopping down beside Cassidy once the coffee shop is vacant again. "What'd I miss?"

"Maci's trying to decide if she should stay here based on fate with her car breaking down, or keep her plan to go to Alaska," Cassidy informs her.

"Oh, fate all the way," Alison says in a *duh* tone.

"That's what I said," Cassidy beams. They share a laugh before eager eyes turn in my direction to await an answer, as if I have it already figured out.

"Like I said, I still need to sort out a car, job, a place to live." I reach for my laptop. "It's not as easy as it sounds."

"Is your baby's father in Alaska?" Alison questions.

I stiffen. My heart rate jumping at the very mention of...*him*.

Duke huffs in frustration, letting his strong arm drop from behind me to wrap around my waist. A firm clasp of his hand settles on my hip and ass. "You don't need to answer that, Maci."

Alison's face heats from Duke's burning glare. "Sorry, I didn't mean to—"

"No, um, it's okay." I pause. How do I put this? "There was an accident, and he, um—" Guilt chokes me once again at the memory of the last time I saw him. I've never seen such anger before. At the time, I didn't understand how a baby could cause such an uproar in our lives. It didn't take long for the missing pieces to fall into answers the next day. "He's...gone."

Shocked expressions stare at me from across the table.

Duke's grip on my hip tightens in a silent form of support, and I find myself leaning into him.

Alison holds a hand to her heart. "You're so brave."

Cassidy shakes her head. "I can't imagine what you're going through. I'm so, so sorry, Maci."

My eyes sting as I look away. Their condolences shouldn't mean as much as they do. I don't deserve them. If they knew the whole truth, would they still say the same? And *brave*? I feel anything but brave.

I sip my mug, needing some form of distraction. "Life throws you punches every now and then," I say, remembering what my grandfather used to tell me. "You have to decide which ones you let knock you down."

Silence settles over the table for a long moment. "But you're pregnant," Cassidy starts, a question in her voice. "What about doctors' appointments and health insurance? What about all your stuff? Is it already in Alaska?"

"I paid my health insurance through the end of next year, and I'm early enough that I don't need to make another appointment until I'm thirteen weeks," I say. "I'll need to pay out-of-network fees until I officially settle somewhere, but it's not much. And my belongings are in a U-Haul container, waiting for my call on where to send it once I'm ready."

Alison gapes. "Wow, you thought of everything."

"Not everything." I shake my head with a forced laugh. "I didn't exactly plan for my car to die on me."

Cassidy smiles wide. "You could've broken down *anywhere*, and you ended up *here*. If that doesn't scream fate, I don't know what does."

"There are two things you don't mess with in life: Mother Nature and Father Fate," Alison sings, like some all-knowing wise owl.

"Did you just make that up?" Cassidy laughs as Alison nods.

A small smile ghosts over my lips when I lift my gaze to Duke. He's already watching me with dark, avid eyes. Warmth spreads throughout my chest, and I wish I knew what he was thinking. Does he think I'm crazy letting fate decide? I feel a little crazy even considering it.

The bell chimes as Butch walks in the door.

Cassidy beams at the sight of him. "Aw, honey, you didn't need to come. I texted you."

He goes right to her, leaning down for a kiss. "I was already on my way. Are you feeling any better?"

"Yes." She smiles, gesturing to me. "Thanks to Maci."

Alison gets up. "Sit, Butch. I've got some cleaning to get done," she says. "You got the front for a bit, Cass?" When she nods, Alison scurries away to the back room.

Butch sits, his gaze flicking between his brother and myself. "Nice to see you again, Maci." His tone *way* friendlier than last night. He shifts his attention beside me. "What you got goin' on today, man?"

Duke glances at me with a slow grin. "Don't know yet."

I bite my lip to keep from smiling. "Well, do you have anything you need to do later today?"

Duke leans back in his seat. "Whatever you're going to ask me will end up what I'm doing. What do you got?"

I scrunch my nose. "Laundry," I say, and he groans. "I need to get some things from my car, too. But the laundromat is a little far, I didn't want to walk—"

"No," he cuts in sternly. "No more walking around today. Not in this cold. Matter of fact, do you own another coat? There are some wind reports coming in for mid-week with a dip in the temp. That worthless coat you got now isn't going to cut it."

This man and his vendetta against my coat. "I only have time for one task today after I finish a little research on *Whitetail, Montana* before my afternoon nausea kicks in. So it's either laundry or coat shopping."

"All right." He scrubs a hand over his scruffy jaw. "We can take your laundry to my mom's. She'll do it while we find you a good winter coat."

Butch chuckles and Cassidy bursts with laughter.

"You're kidding, right?" I say in disbelief. He can't actually think that's a solution. "Duke, I am *not* taking my dirty underwear to your mother for her to wash for me. I don't even know her. And please, *please* tell me you don't still take your dirty clothes to your parents' house."

He scowls across the table at the laughing duo. "There's no washer and dryer at the rental cabin," he adds in an attempt to defend himself. "So, yeah, I take it to Ma's so I don't have to pay at the laundromat. She doesn't mind. Folds it and everything."

I raise a brow. "Seriously, Duke, how old are you?"

"He's thirty-three." Butch chuckles deeply. "He'll be thirty-four in February."

"Shut it, Butch," Duke huffs. "You used to wait until you didn't have a single clean piece of clothing left before you did yours, then Cassidy came around to do it for you. You'd go out and buy a whole pack of new boxers just so you didn't have to wash any. And don't even act like you didn't, 'cause you told me that yourself."

Butch glares at his brother.

"Aw, babe," Cassidy coos, leaning into him. "And you tried to give me a hard time that first day we lived together. Like you really wanted to do it yourself."

Duke scoffs. "He fooled your ass, Cassidy. He was more excited about you doing his laundry than you cooking dinner."

"All right, that's enough," Butch grumbles. Cassidy laughs, pecking him on the cheek. The second she does, his scowl diminishes, and he's wrapping an arm around her like she's the most important woman in the world. And to him, she probably is.

I sigh at the sight.

Duke tugs at my hip, and I look up from his side. His rough, manly cologne floods my senses and sends a dampening heat right between my thighs.

And at the crooked grin on his lips, I know what—or *who*—I'm doing later.

Twelve.

Duke

Me: *Was the rest of that sub enough for you for dinner?*

Maci: *Yup. How's Sunday dinner going at your parents'?*

"Is that Maci?" Cassidy beams from across the extended dining table at my parents' house.

I don't know why her curiosity about Maci annoys me so much, but it does. *You want her all to yourself, you fool.*

After spending a few hours at the coffee shop with Maci while she looked into staying here in Whitetail, I took her shopping for a new coat. It wasn't exactly how I planned on spending my Sunday afternoon, but I'd be lying if I said I didn't have a blast with her.

Our conversations flowed effortlessly—talking, joking, laughing about anything and everything. Every quirk she was revealing about herself had me taking note—she hates cashews and bottled water from *Aquafina* and something about the side guy from *You* gives her the creeps.

She has no idea I'm falling for her with every word.

After we found her a heavy coat that can last a Montana winter, I dropped her off at the motel to rest. I wanted to invite her tonight—I'd thought about it all day—but that little voice in my head just kept screaming; *no strings attached.*

What if I want those strings?

I'm getting the sense she's trying to keep me at arm's length. And I hate it. It grates under my skin like a knife. I've told her countless times to call me with anything she needs, and she's still not listening. What do I have to do for her to let me take care of her?

I shouldn't care this much. We've known each other for barely three days, she's pregnant with another man's baby, we hooked up once... Yet, here I am, missing her the second I dropped her off.

"Yeah."

"Tell her I talked to Peggy, and we're definitely looking for more help at the coffee shop," Cassidy says, adding, "It'd only be part-time until the second location opens in a few months, but it's something. Alison also called around about yoga classes. They don't offer them at Rick's Gym, but they were really interested in starting something like that."

My brow furrows. "Did she ask you to look into that for her?"

"No, but—"

"Then back off," I deadpan. I want her to stay on her own accord, not because other people are pushing for it. I want her to *want* to stay. With me.

Butch scowls. "What the hell is your deal, man? I thought you liked this chick."

"Isn't she pregnant?" Levi burps out.

The room goes silent as every pair of Montgomery eyes lands on me.

"Who's pregnant?" Lily, my sister, is the first to ask. Unlike the rest of the Montgomery men with dark hair and eyes, Lily is a blonde-haired, blue-eyed, ex-model. Similar to Levi, she enjoys watching her brothers squirm in the hot seat.

"Why didn't you invite her tonight?" Rhett asks, shoveling in a forkful of pasta. "Ma always makes too much."

"Who are we talkin' 'bout?" my father asks, taking a swig of his beer.

"No one, Pop," I say sternly, my gaze sliding around the table in warning.

Butch glares at me, crossing his arms over his chest. That son of a— "Maci Baker," he starts. My fist tightens around my fork in hand. "Duke helped her out a few nights ago. She was just passing through, and got stranded. Now she's thinking about staying if she can find a job."

"Well, that's nice of you, dear," my mother says kindly.

"So, what's her story?" Lily asks curiously, handing Parker his drink. "She was just passing through? To where?"

"Her story is *wild*, Lily," Cassidy beams, catching everyone's attention.

"Yeah, and it's her story to tell," I grind out. I doubt Maci would like the idea of everyone in town knowing her business. I sure as hell don't. And between Lily, Cassidy, Levi, and my mother—everyone will. "Maybe you should leave it at that."

Cassidy frowns, shoulders dropping. Butch's jaw clenches as he pushes back in his chair to stand. "You got a fuckin' problem, Duke, speak up."

I toss my fork down with a clang and stand to counter his posture. "Yeah, I fuckin' do. Keep your fiancée out of my goddamn business."

"Duke, I wasn't trying to—" Cassidy tries to say, but is cut off by my growling brother stalking around the table to meet me.

Bring it on, asshole. I've been itching to clear this heat with him. It's about time we settled it like how we used to when we were younger. Levi and Rhett jump up, picking a brother and attempting to hold us back from throwing down right here in the dining room.

"Enough," Ma snaps. "Sit your asses down now, both of you."

Doing as we're told, we sit. Glaring at one another like we're feuding in middle school over who gets to be team captain in gym class. Just one good hit to his smug face would set my nerves to rest.

"I'm sorry," Cass says quietly. "I wasn't trying to cause any problems between you and Maci."

"Oh my god, are you *dating* someone?" Lily blurts, loud and shocked.

I grit my teeth. I'm done.

The back of my chair hits the ground in an echoing *smack* of wood hitting wood. I don't intend to stick around and listen to the next generation of gossiping Betty's ready to take over Whitetail alongside my prick of a brother. I storm out of the dining room to the sound of my family calling me back, but I don't stop. I stalk down the hall to the front door, yank on my boots, grab my jacket, and head for my truck.

I drive straight to Whitetail Motel. When my phone rings with calls and dings with texts, I only check to be sure it isn't Maci needing me.

At this point, it's more like I need her.

I park my truck in front of her room and kill the engine. I'm pounding a heavy fist on her door a second later. *I swear, if she's not in here...*

The slide of the chain lock and twist of the deadbolt has me blowing out the hot air boiling in my lungs.

"Duke?" Maci says, confused and beautiful in a pair of floral pajama pants and a white long-sleeve. No bra. "What are you—"

I hoist her up by her ass in one smooth motion as I step inside. She wraps her legs around my waist and locks her delicate arms around my neck. "In this room, you're mine, remember?" I growl. She nods without hesitation as the door closes behind me. "I missed you, angel."

My lips crash against hers. Her tongue slips into my mouth as her body presses flush against me. Our mouths twist and caress—every kiss with her is fuel to my addiction for this girl.

She pulls away for those emerald eyes to search my face. She's smart. She knows there's more to what's going on within me than I'm letting on—needing her like this, calling her angel, showing up just to tell her I missed her.

I kick off my boots by the door and carry her to the bed where she's got her laptop open and a notepad beside it. "What were you doing?" I ask as I set her on the edge to take off my jacket.

"Working out some details," she says, scooting farther onto the bed and crossing her legs beneath her. "Is everything okay?"

I shrug. "Yes. No. Somewhere in between."

She bites her lip as I tug my sweatshirt over my head, the shirt underneath riding up to expose my lower abdomen. I flex under her hungry stare. "What details were you working out?"

"Nothing important." She closes the laptop and sets it off to the side with her notes. "Did you want to talk about—"

I'd rather talk about *her*. "What details?" I ask again, sitting on the edge of the bed.

She huffs, eyeing me before she says, "The details on me staying."

My heart is in my throat, and I fight to swallow it down. *She's staying.* "You've decided?"

Maci looks down at her hands in her lap. "I'm not sure I have a choice," she admits. "They rescinded the job offer in Anchorage, and with the cost of living being so high there... It wouldn't be smart to keep to my original plan. It took weeks of begging to land that job in the first place." She shakes her head. "I should've known it would fall through before I even got there."

"Cassidy said there's a part-time job open at the coffee shop for you if you want it," I say. "And Rick's Gym is open to starting yoga classes."

"Really?" She perks up. "When did she say that? I just emailed that gym not even ten minutes ago."

"Alison and Cass called around earlier for you."

Maci rolls her eyes. "Nosey bodies."

I scoff. "You have no idea."

Her smile falters as I fall back on the bed, my feet still on the floor. "So, um, not to sound rude or anything," she says, "but...why are you here? Did something happen?"

I sigh heavily and rub my face. "Butch just knows how to get under my skin. I love the bastard, but fuck, sometimes he makes it impossible to be around him. And Cass was pissing me off with butting into your business. She's got a big mouth, Maci, I should've warned you beforehand."

She sighs, looking away.

I sit up and reach for her. Bringing her to straddle my lap, I hold her to me as I move up the bed, sitting with my back against the headboard. "I know you want to be in a place where no one knows your story, but would you tell me?"

Her hands brace against my chest as she eyes me warily. "Why does it matter?"

I slide my hands over her hips and thighs, up and down in an attempt to soothe the worry in her eyes. "Is it selfish of me if I say I don't want to hear it from anyone but you?" I ask, and when she remains skeptical, I add, "Everything said and done between us is kept between us, Maci. I can promise you that. And I hope you'll grant me that same respect."

"Of course, I will."

"Good." I let my head fall back. "'Cause I'm going to be honest with you right now, the reason Butch and I have been butting heads is because he's getting married and starting a family," I tell her. My eyes close on a cringe. "Fuck. When I say it out loud, it sounds even worse."

The soothing feel of her hand gliding over mine has me forcing the words out. "I was married once. Her name was Rachel. She and three others died in a plane crash just over five years ago."

Her hold tightens on my hand. "I'm so sorry."

I grip her hips, staying in the moment with her. "Don't be. It happened a long time ago," I say. "And now, with everything going on between their upcoming wedding and baby. I don't know... It's hitting me in a way I'm not proud of."

"Why do you think that is?"

I shrug. "He's happy and I'm not."

Her head tilts slightly. "You're jealous?"

"The short answer is yes."

She raises a brow. "What's the long answer?"

I take in a deep breath and continue massaging her thighs. "Enough about me. It's your turn," I say instead, deflecting when I know I shouldn't. "Tell me why you left Oklahoma."

She sighs, leaning away from me to grab her phone off the nightstand. I wait as she swipes and scrolls—for what, I'm not sure. She holds the phone up with a news article on the screen dated two months ago: *Governor's Son-in-Law Dead, Is his Mistress to Blame?*

"What the hell is this?" I say as I take the phone from her hand and start to read. My eyes widen when I stop on a picture of a petite woman hiding her face as she leaves a police station. Long waves of deep, auburn-red hair flash outside of a grey ball cap.

"I didn't know he was married," she finally says. "Evan was...really good at lying." She huffs a forced laugh. "We were together for about eight months or so. He told me he was in real estate—you know, the whole 'travel for work' excuse. And, well, I trusted him more than I should've at the time." Her shoulders sag as she looks away. "When I found out I was pregnant, I was happy. Excited at the idea of us moving forward...the three of us." She swipes a stray tear from her cheek, steeling her spine. "Evan didn't feel the same, of course. He, um, was angry I wanted to keep the baby, and...things were said. He left, and the next morning his face was all over the news. He'd gotten drunk—something the news articles don't mention—and was driving recklessly to the point he rolled his car and died at the scene."

My gaze shifts to the phone screen once more. "And they thought you had something to do with it?"

"He was the governor's son-in-law," she says. "There had to be an investigation. People wanted answers. Someone to blame..." She sighs. "I started getting death threats from all over the state. Some thought I was working to bring the governor down. Ridiculous accusations." She shakes her head as more tears fall. "People can be...awful when they want to be."

I toss the phone aside and guide her to me. She falls over me, burying her face into my chest. "I lost my job at a reputable yoga studio. My parents disowned me. My friends blocked my calls. There was nothing left for me to do but leave. So I did."

"What did they say when you told them you're pregnant?" I ask.

Maci sits up then with a somber expression. "They don't know," she confesses before clenching her eyes shut as she starts to cry.

I hold her face in my hands. "Maci." Opening her eyes, she places her delicate hand over mine on her cheek, my heart paining with the hurt in their emerald depths. "I'm sorry you had to go through that, angel."

"I'm okay," she whispers, nearly inaudible. Unable to stop the tears. "*We* are okay. I'm starting over. That's all that matters."

"You're going to be an amazing mother," I tell her, and I mean it. She's the strongest, most genuine person I've ever known.

A slow smile spreads across her face. "Thank you." She leans in to place a tender kiss on my lips. When she pulls away, she bites her lip anxiously. "So, um, not to be one of *those* people, but—"

"Anything you need, darlin'." I grin.

"It's three things, actually." She giggles as I raise a brow in question. "First, I found a few used cars in my price range, I was wondering if you would give me your thoughts? Maybe come with me to see them this week?"

"No problem," I say. "I'll help you trade or sell your car, too. Whatever you plan on doing." I lift my chin. "What else?"

"Well," she starts, running her hands down my chest with a light scrape of her nails through the thin fabric of my shirt. "I was wondering..." she trails off, and I grin.

My cock pulses to life beneath her lush little ass. "You don't even need to ask," I growl, my hands trail under her shirt and around her back. Soft, silky skin under rough, calloused palms.

"It's, um, more than that," she adds with a hint of uncertainty.

My smile fades momentarily. "What is it, Maci?"

"I'm pregnant. And, well, pregnant women have...*extra* needs." She laughs at her words, and I find myself grinning. "I guess what I'm trying to ask is if you'll be my friend-with-benefits while I'm pregnant. I know we've only known each other for a few days, but I trust you, and that's a big deal for me. And, seven months from now, when I'm big, round, and miserable, begging someone to have sex with me so I can jump-start labor. I'd prefer that someone be you."

I raise a brow. "Begging, huh?"

She rolls her eyes with a smile. "Is that a yes?"

I move fast, holding her tight to me as I flip her beneath me with her back pressed into the mattress. She laughs as I grind my hardening cock against her. "That's a fuck yes, but just to be clear, we'll be doing this *exclusively*. No one else. You and me. That's it."

She nods.

My chest tightens as hope and fear and joy crash into me all at once. "Then I want this to feel real when we're together, doll."

Her brow furrows as she studies me. "Duke, I—"

"I'm not asking it to *be* real. I'm asking for it to *feel* real. I've been miserable for so long. These last few days being with you... Damnit, baby, I'm fucking happy."

Her smile is weak as she snakes her arms around my neck. "I like spending time with you, too."

I dip my head into the crook of her neck and inhale deeply. "What else did you need, beautiful? You said it was three things. What's the third?" I ask, laying a tender kiss on her shoulder.

"Ice cream."

I chuckle, leaning away to stare down at her gorgeous smile. "You want ice cream?"

"The *baby* wants ice cream," she says teasingly.

I back down her body and push her shirt up to expose her small, round bump. I rub a gentle hand over her stomach, a warmth in my heart as she places her hand over mine. "Anything either of you need, I'm here. For both of you," I say to her, meaning every word of it.

A single tear rolls down her cheek.

I kiss her bump and tug on the waistband of her bottoms. "Ice cream or orgasms." I grin smugly. "Which do you want first?"

With a sexy spark in her eye, she lifts her hips in response. I yank her pants and panties off and toss them to the side. Nudging her thighs apart, I take in the sight of her pretty, damp pussy.

"Be gentle," she says. "I'm still a little sore."

I kiss her thighs softly, earning a breathy moan from her. "Don't worry, sweetheart. I'll take real good care of you." I groan, kissing her core before I give her a long, slow lick over her clit—loving her taste, her smell, every goddamn thing about her.

And she's all mine.

Thirteen.

Maci

WITH MY PUSSY STILL pulsing from back-to-back orgasms, Duke positions himself behind me. He yanks my hips where he wants them with a playful smack on my ass. "Duke," I moan, dying to have him inside me. I fist the sheets to hold myself in place as he surges forward—filling me with a delicious ache.

"Fuck," he grunts, gripping my ass as he slowly pumps his cock deeper and deeper with each thrust. He slams into me hard enough to make my legs shake. My body arches as he pounds me into a third orgasm. "That's it, baby," he growls, reaching around to rub my throbbing clit.

I push back and grind my hips, forcing his cock to brush against my G-spot. "Yes, right there. Yes, Duke." I gasp as he fucks me harder, faster. Pressing me down, he continues to glide his shaft against my core how I need him to.

Unable to muffle my screams, my entire body trembles with a hard, long release. Duke fucks me mercilessly through it. "Fuuuck," he groans, grunting in time with the slap of his hips against my ass.

He comes buried deep inside of me, his fingers digging into my hips to keep me in place as his cock twitches into my throbbing pussy. He pumps his cock slowly for a moment before gently pulling out.

I flop to the side, a panting, orgasm-induced mess as my legs continue to shake. Duke lays down beside me, breathing heavily with a smug grin plastered on his face. "You all right?"

My smile is goofy and far too wide. "Yes."

He chuckles, engulfing me in his strong arms as we lay naked together. I snuggle into him, placing my hand on his broad chest peppered with short, dark hair. His heart races beneath my palm. "What kind of ice cream do you want?" he asks finally, breaking the euphoric sex haze.

I laugh, nuzzling into his chest with a yawn. "I'll know when I see it."

He kisses my forehead. "I'd rather you stay here," he says. "I'll go so you don't have to deal with the cold."

"Are you sure?" I sit up and scoot to the edge of the bed to stand, but my legs have other plans. I plop back down and laugh, peering over my shoulder at a man soaking up the clear ego boost.

"Hang on." He grins, coming around to help me to the bathroom.

"You know, this happened last time," I say.

"Oh, yeah?" He loops a strong arm around my naked waist as my trembling legs fail to cooperate.

"I had to hold on to the wall. You were too busy snoring like a broken fan to help."

He throws his head back with a laugh. "I only snore when I'm on my back," he protests. "If you give me a hard shove, I'll roll on my side. Shuts me right up."

He leans into the shower and turns it on. We step into the tight space together, and he holds me close as the hot water runs over us. He gathers a dollop of body wash and starts to lather me, seeming to take extra care over my stomach.

"I think it's a girl," I whisper.

Duke pauses his movements, his dark eyes finding mine. "What makes you say that?"

I smile. "Just a feeling."

"When do you get to find out?" he asks, his hand covered in suds sliding between my thighs with even more care.

"At twenty weeks," I say. "I'd love to go to one of those 3D ultrasound places, but I doubt you have one around here."

"Not here, but I'm sure Helena has a place."

I scrunch my nose. "Helena?"

He chuckles. "It's the capital of Montana."

"Oh." I guess I better learn a few more things about this place before I fully settle.

Duke gets dressed while I slip into my pajamas and under the covers. I flick on the TV when he decides to just run across the street to the gas station for the ice cream. "Where's your room key?" he asks, tugging on his coat.

I point to my purse. "Front pocket."

He takes the room key and leans down for a kiss. "You want me to text you a picture or call you?"

"Picture."

He kisses me again, firmer this time. "I'll be right back."

My belly flip-flops like a love-struck teen watching him head out the door to fetch my craving. Never, in all my twenty-six years, has a man waited on me or remotely cared what I wanted. Now here is a man who gets a spark in his eye when I ask him for a favor like it's a gift I'm giving him.

Duke might be one in a million.

Too bad I'm a mess of pregnant baggage. *Why couldn't I have met him before?*

And his confession of being a widower... His face when he opened up about the tension between him and his brother—his need for us to feel real—was heartbreaking. For everything he's been doing for me, and continues to do, giving him this one thing is the least I can do.

Let's just hope I can keep my feelings in check.

Duke: *[Image]*

Duke: *This is all they got. See anything you like?*

Me: *Panda Paws, please.*

Duke: *You want two? They're only in pint size.*

Me: *Just one for me is fine.*

Duke: *You got it, gorgeous.*

I smile, watching the door and counting the seconds until he returns. *Didn't I just say I should keep my feelings in check?* I'm a lost cause.

—ele—

I don't know when I fell asleep—well, probably while Duke was rambling on about car stuff—but when I wake up, the room is dark and there's a strong arm pinning me against a warm chest.

He stayed.

I slide my hand over his, interlocking our fingers as I listen to his light wheeze of a snore. My eyes well with tears. I didn't expect him to stay a second night in a row. I sniffle, wiping my tears away. I don't even know why I'm crying over this. I wanted him to stay.

Duke nuzzles into the crook of my neck, his hot breath fanning me as he lays a kiss below my ear. His hand slides away from mine to rest over my stomach, his thumb gently rubbing soothing circles.

If I hadn't already decided to stay, that small action alone would've sealed my fate.

Fourteen.

Duke

I STAND WITH MY arms crossed over my chest while Maci looks over the used, but new, Ford Explorer. It's got winter tires, low miles, good gas mileage, all-wheel-drive, a family-grade vehicle with a five-star crash test rating, and it's available in blue or red—which is also very important, apparently.

She thinks they lowered the price by five grand, but what she doesn't know, is I called ahead to the salesman early this morning. Based on everything she showed me last night in her price range, I know she's trying to keep her payments low. But I've got the money. And giving a chunk of change for a car that'll keep her and the baby safe seems like a damn good investment to me. I've looked this thing over with a fine-tooth comb—it's in great shape for the price they're (now) asking.

"What do you think?" I ask.

"It's nice," she says, sitting in the driver's seat. She's already test-driven it, and I can tell she likes it, but she doesn't seem sold. "Why do you think they lowered the price?"

I shrug. "They're getting in new inventory. End of the year sort of thing."

Maci nods as the salesman, Steve, who I used to go to high school with, strides over with a bright smile. "So, what's the verdict?" he asks, playing along just like I told him to.

I raise a brow at Maci staring at me with nervous doe eyes. "It's a good deal. And a damn good car to be riding around in with the baby."

"Baby?" Steve beams. "Congratulations, you two. I didn't know."

Maci's face twists uncomfortably. "Um, thanks. Anyway, what, uh, is the down payment?"

I knew she'd ask this. Which is why I told Steve to tell her a low-ball offer. I don't know her financial situation, but from what I can tell, she's trying to conserve. Whether that's for rent or baby stuff—probably both.

Maci decides to make the deal, and if I could fist bump the air—or Steve—without looking suspicious, I would. We go through the motions of trading her old car in. Unfortunately, with her having to switch her plates to Montana and no current address, she's looking at a hold-up on the deal.

"You can use my address," I tell her when Steve walks away to check with someone about her out-of-state driver's license.

"Are you sure?" she asks, scrunching her nose in the way I adore.

I throw my arm behind her chair and jerk her closer. "Yes," I say, kissing her possessively. It takes me a moment to get a grip and realize we're in a public place. But Maci doesn't miss a beat or question my actions, she falls into me, kissing me back with just as much heat.

We part, and she leans into me with a smile. "Thank you."

After Maci signs on the dotted line and we make plans to pick up her new car tomorrow afternoon. Hand in hand we walk to my truck when she gets a phone call. "Hello?" I hold the door for her to climb in, unable to help myself from smacking her ass as she does. Her swat back at me has me chuckling before I jog around to get in the driver's seat. "Really? When? Yes, I'll be there. Thank you so much, Cassidy. I will. Bye."

"What'd she say?" I ask when she hangs up.

"Peggy Cup, the owner of Cup O' Joe, asked if I could come in to meet her tomorrow morning," she says, checking her email for the third time in the last hour.

I pull out and head toward the shop so we can clear out her car. "That's a good thing, right?"

"Yeah, I mean, it is." She sighs. "It's just... None of these apartments are getting back to me. They all said 'move-in ready' and 'available now,' but no one is returning my call."

"It's still early in the week. You only reached out to them yesterday," I try to assure her as she drops her phone into her purse. "So, where do you want to take your stuff? The motel?"

"I don't have anywhere else to take it yet."

Coming to a stop at a red light, I rub my face and ponder the best way to approach this with her. "It's Monday."

"Yes, it is." She giggles.

I grin. "No, angel, it's *Monday*. You only have the room until Wednesday."

"Thursday, technically," she corrects. "I have to be checked out of there by Thursday morning at the latest."

"All right, well, that's not leaving you a lot of time to be out of there," I say. "You need a backup plan if nothing comes through."

"Are there any other motels around here?"

"No. You're at the only one in town," I grunt. "There's the hotel at the resort, but their prices are high due to the holiday season." Maci puts a protective hand over her stomach, a telltale sign she's getting upset. "If you can't find a place by Wednesday, you can stay with me at the rental cabin."

She leans her head against the seat. "I can't ask you to do that, Duke. I'm a big girl, I'll figure it out."

She's missing the point. I wasn't asking. "I won't sit by and watch you stress over finding a place in three days when I've got room. It's not good for you, or the baby."

"Duke..."

"Maci," I warn, regarding her and her defensive tone. She won't win this fight with me. If I have to drag her suitcase with her attached to it, I will. "We've spent the last two nights together. You'll have a car tomorrow to get wherever you need to go. It's a one-bedroom, one-bathroom cabin. It's not much, but you'll be with me, and...it's somewhere safe," I add, my chest tied up in knots.

Safe.

That damnable word...

"You're sure that's a good idea?" she asks quietly.

"Why wouldn't it be?"

She frowns. "Two words: four days."

"And?" I scoff. "I trust you not to smother me in my sleep. We get along great. I sleep better than I have in years when I'm with you. So, no, I don't see the problem. Actually, I think it's a damn good idea."

Her emerald gaze softens. "Is that why you stayed last night?"

I huff, glancing at her, then back to the road. No sense in denying it now. "Yeah. I love being in that bed with you—no matter what we're doing. I like...having you close."

A teasing smile blooms across her lips. "You don't snore when you're on your side, but you do this weird wheeze." She giggles. "Also, there's no such thing as shoving you over. You're a boulder when you sleep."

I boom with laughter. "Fuck, really? A *wheeze*?"

"Yes." She laughs. "It's not bad, but you could use those nighttime nasal strips that open your nose better. They'd probably help."

"All right, fine, if I get the nasal strips, you'll come stay with me then?" I don't want to push her too hard, but I need to know so I can ask my mom to clean the place beforehand.

Don't judge.

"Only if you let me pay you something for staying with you," she counters, and I grin. "Not in blow jobs either." My smile fades. "Please. I don't like handouts, and you've already done so much for me these last few days."

I pull into the diner down the street and park. "Fine, but I'm buying lunch. And whatever craving you have on request tonight."

"Are you...staying again tonight?" she asks.

"Do you want me to?" I'll sleep outside her door in my truck to be close to her if I have to.

She leans over the center console and pouts her plump lips at me. My cock surges at the visual of pushing my length between those lips. "Yes, please," she whispers seductively, and I fall toward her. Claiming her mouth in a searing kiss. I don't think my heart has ever soared higher.

Maci Montgomery.

Has a nice ring to it, doesn't it?

After working late at the shop, I crashed hard at the motel with Maci. She wasn't feeling well, but I was more than glad to take care of her. I offered to take her to the coffee shop to meet Peggy in the morning, but Cassidy already said she'd swing by and get her on the way.

We texted all day, but that didn't curb my desire to see her—to be with her. After skipping out of work early, we picked up her new car. She was much more excited about it, but she still seemed upset over the apartment search being a dud—I, however, am *not*.

I stayed with her again last night at the motel. We had amazing sex in the shower and went to bed like we'd been together for years.

She started training at Cup O' Joe this morning, had a meeting with Rick at Rick's Gym this afternoon about starting yoga classes, then headed to the laundromat before we meet to head up to the cabin in another hour—it's finally Wednesday, and I can't wait to get her moved in.

Maci's eleven weeks pregnant as of yesterday, and doing some quick math, I've figured her due date is roughly the end of June. I'll be in my house no later than the end of May at the rate Rhett and Levi are going; that's enough time to convince Maci to give us a real shot.

Dating isn't on her radar, and I doubt starting a serious relationship while throwing a newborn baby into the mix is something she's going to be keen on doing, but I have to try. We're already there as far as I'm concerned.

I want her. And I want that baby *with* her.

I want it all.

A heavy knock on my open office door brings me back to the present. "Hey," Butch grunts. "Got a minute?"

I glare at him and lean back in my desk chair, remembering the last time I saw him and how well that went.

He takes the seat across from me and scratches his bearded chin—a nervous tick he's had since grade school. "Listen, Duke, I didn't mean to piss you off the other night at Ma's," he grumbles, "but I don't like where we've gotten. I'm a fish out of water here, all right? You're the one who fixes this shit before we end up ripping each other's throats out."

"Yeah, I always am," I snarl. "How's it being on the other end? Not very fun, is it?"

Butch scowls. "I didn't come here to argue with you."

"Then why did you come here?" I ask, crossing my arms over my chest. "To find out what the fuck I'm doing with *my* goddamn life and report back to the family."

"No." He sighs. "I came here to invite you and Maci over for dinner Friday night. Cassidy already tried talking to Maci about it, but she said she'd have to talk to you. Didn't want to step on any toes or some bullshit."

I huff in frustration.

"Cass likes Maci," he tells me. "And apparently, I'm fucking up her chance at having a pregnant best friend she can go through all this shit with, and that's a big deal."

I can't help but chuckle at my moron of a brother. It's a wonder how he scored Cassidy in the first place. "Yeah, that'll do it."

"So, you'll come?" he asks, hopeful. "Dinner, Friday night."

As much as I'd enjoy watching him squirm in the dog house with his future wife, I'd hate to find out later I'm doing the same thing to Maci. "I'll be there," I say. "I can't guarantee Maci will, but I'll talk to her."

He nods. "Sounds good."

I rub the back of my neck as something else comes to mind... "What did you end up getting Cassidy for Christmas?"

He barks a laugh. "I was about to ask you the same thing. If I was smart, I would've waited to ask her to marry me on Christmas. Killed two birds with one stone."

I snort at his cheap ass. "Yeah, I don't know if I should get Maci something or not."

"You're not dating, are you?"

"We're...a little more than friends," I admit, hoping I don't regret telling him later. "It's been so long since I had to buy a woman anything with meaning, I don't even know where I'd start."

We hem and haw for a few minutes, neither of us coming up with anything good. "Jewelry is always the way to go, right?" my brother asks.

I shrug. "For you, that'd work. Earrings or whatever. I doubt I could get away without that gettin' taken the wrong way."

Butch stands. "Nice. Well, thanks for the help, bro. I've got some earrings to find."

"Hey." I throw my hands up. "Where the hell is *my* brotherly advice?"

"Don't look at me. I don't fall for fuck buddies. That's all you, brother," he says with a smirk, strolling out the door. "See you Friday."

Asshole.

I grab my keys and close up. Five minutes later, I'm at the motel catching Maci walking out with a bag in hand. Her smile lights up at the sight of me, and it hits me like a shot to the heart. I jump out and stalk toward her, taking the bag first. "Hey," I say, leaning down for a kiss—not caring who sees. "This everything?"

"Almost," she says, blushing even in the cold.

I load the rest of her belongings and the few groceries she's gathered through the week, then have her follow my lead up the mountain to one of Beau's two rental cabins. I park out front of the smaller cabin, a quaint covered porch that matches the one on the back. The cabin next door is twice the size with the same rustic, mountain vacation feel.

I unlock the door, and we step inside with a flick of the overhead light.

To the left is the small kitchen-dining area and a sliding glass door that leads to the back porch. The four-seater table feeds into the living space where there's a couch and a coffee table across from the stone fireplace. To the right is the bedroom where I've somehow crammed in a king-sized bed, a dresser, and a flatscreen setup. The tight bathroom is attached to the bedroom from there.

I wonder how she's going to feel when she sees there's no door to the bathroom—or all the red flannel and black bear décor my mother decorated this place with.

"This is cute," Maci says, looking around.

"Bedroom is through there," I say, pointing to the open doorway. "I'll get the rest of your stuff." Once everything is inside, I start putting away the groceries while she organizes her things.

"Where's the bathroom door?" she shouts from the bedroom, mortified.

I chuckle to myself as she comes back out and stares at me, waiting for an answer.

"Duke," she says. "We *need* a bathroom door."

"I know, I know," I huff. "Ma already chewed my ass for not telling her it broke a few months back."

"How'd it break?" she asks, wheeling her luggage into the bedroom.

"I fell into it," I reply. "Tripped on the bathmat."

Her faint laugh drifts from the other room. "There is no bathmat."

"I threw it in the closet." I grin. "I'll get Rhett or Levi out here to fix it sometime next week."

Maci comes out of the bedroom, hanging up her coat on the hook by the door—right next to mine. Where her boots are neatly set off to the side—right next to mine. *Fuck, this feels good.*

While she's in the shower, I move a few things between my dresser and the closet, trying to clear space for her. If she feels welcome, she'll stay, right? *She's not a dog, you moron.* Doesn't hurt to try.

"Did you want to go to dinner at Butch and Cassidy's on Friday?" I ask when she steps into the bedroom to get dressed—a single towel wrapped around her sexy frame, hair dripping wet.

My cock weeps with joy that she's here. And all mine.

"We don't have to go if you don't want—" She squeaks as I snatch the towel away, her hands flying to cup her breasts. As if I haven't worshiped them countless times in the last few days. "Duke!"

I drop the towel and scoop her up. Her laughter a soothing melody to my aching heart. "Have I told you how happy I am that you're here?" I growl, laying her down on my bed. I kneel on the edge and lean over her, my fists on either side of her head as she gazes up at me with lustful eyes.

"You haven't showered yet," she whispers as I brush a damp strand of hair from her face. I trail her features, absorbing this moment and committing it to memory.

I dip to her lips and leave a feather-light kiss. A breathy moan escapes her as she slides her arms around my neck. "I…" My mouth works before my right mind has time to catch up. Words I haven't spoken in years lodge in my throat like an anchor.

Don't say it, my past warns. *No good can come from it.*
It's too soon.

"...should shower," I say instead. *Pussy.*

There's a small crease between her brow as she watches me—knows me. I've never been good with hiding my emotions like my brothers—Butch and Beau are the experts in that department.

She nods, pulling me in for another lingering kiss before I stand and force my legs to move away from her while she gets ready for bed.

The pounding heat and clouding steam from the shower aid to block out the war going on inside my head. What I feel—real versus lust. What's coincidence over what's meant to be...

Fate, I stubbornly recall.

If I didn't know any better, I'd say I'm starting to believe it.

Maci

"I THINK YOU'VE POPPED, Maci," Alison announces, staring at my belly.

"Did you?" Cassidy gasps, rushing out of the back room.

I laugh, wiping down the front counter of Cup O' Joe—my new part-time job. After an unwelcome interview with Rick's Gym—who found my current 'situation' unmanageable in the long run, Duke suggested I contact Winton's Resort on the mountain. It proved to be a night-and-day experience. The manager at Winton's was eager to jump on my offer of private, couple, and group yoga classes—not rude in the slightest when I told them I was pregnant.

And the classes have been going great: Every Thursday and Friday are reserved for regular group classes, while Saturdays are for couples. Three, forty-five-minute classes with a fifteen-minute break in between to start—and they're already asking to add two more to the schedule. That's how fast the classes are filling up.

It's a dream come true.

My string of bad luck seems to have finally ended. *Fingers crossed*.

I've been living with Duke at the rental cabin for two weeks, and I *still* haven't heard a peep about any available apartments in Whitetail. I even went out of my price range and still nothing.

Cassidy says it's because they're all being used as vacation rentals for the holiday season, that after the new year, she thinks I'll get a call.

Not that I'm overly eager to leave the cabin. Living with Duke has been...another dream. We don't fight, we don't argue, and every day he goes out of his way to make me feel special—whether it's a text or call just to see how I'm feeling, bringing me lunch or my pre-packed snacks to work for me because I forgot them.

He's the kind of man women only read about in books.

The only downside—if you can call it that—is he hasn't let me pay him anything for staying. Instead, he's been asking me for menial favors, like helping him pick out flooring for the house build, cabinets, countertops, and even exterior siding. Don't get me wrong, we have a blast doing it—joking and making fun of carpet samples that should be named after different shades of dog poop.

We've spent every day and every night together. And I fear my feelings for Duke are starting to take on a whole new meaning. Because these last two and a half weeks with him have been nothing short of perfect.

Being thirteen weeks pregnant, and officially in my second trimester, it's hard to say if it's the hormones or that every time Duke rubs my belly I want to cry, jump on him, run away, and proclaim my undying love for him all at once.

"Duke said the same thing," I say to Alison regarding my growing bump.

Cassidy stands beside me, pulling her matching Cup O' Joe work shirt tight over her belly. "What do you think, Al?" she asks. "Who's bigger? I'll be ten weeks tomorrow."

Alison grabs her phone and starts snapping pictures. "Show me those babies!" We laugh, proceeding to push our tiny bumps together.

When Duke and I went to dinner at Butch and Cassidy's a few weeks ago, Duke thought we'd be leaving early to avoid a fight. But it turned into a nice evening. It was clear afterwards that the stubborn brothers' relationship is on the mend.

"When did you say your appointment is with Dr. Sanderson?" Cassidy asks, smiling at the pictures Alison just sent her.

"I have to be there by 11:30 AM," I reply, checking the time. "I should probably get going actually."

The bell above the door chimes, and Duke strolls in.

My brow furrows for a moment before a smile splits my face. "Hey, what are you doing here?"

He grins, walking straight toward me. "Your appointment is today, right?"

"Yes, but..."

"Oh, good. I'm glad you're going with her, Duke. Those offices by the hospital can be so confusing. They all look the same," Cassidy says.

Alison hands me my purse and jacket from the back. "We'll see you tomorrow for couple's yoga," she exclaims with a giddy bounce. "Tanner can't wait."

I tug on my coat and say a quick goodbye before following Duke out to the parking lot. "I'll drive," he says, resting a firm hand on my lower back, steering us in the direction of his truck.

I open my mouth to protest, but I'm so confused, I can't form the words. We're halfway to the doctor's office when I turn to him. "What are you doing?"

"Driving you to your appointment," he says, glancing at me, then to the road.

My gaze narrows. "Why are you driving me to my appointment? We never talked about you picking me up."

He shrugs. "I took an early lunch. Figured we could get something to eat after."

It's innocent enough, sure, but I feel like I've come to know my friends-with-benefits-temporary-roommate fairly well these last few weeks. "Is something wrong?" I ask. "Oh, no. Did Joey put laxatives in your coffee again?"

Duke shakes his head with a chuckle. "That fucker better never do that shit again if he wants to keep his job," he says. "And no, angel, nothing's wrong. I just...want to go with you, make sure you get there okay. Is that all right?"

His hand finds mine resting on the center console, and he laces his thick, calloused fingers through mine. Heat and a familiar comfort radiate from his palm to mine. "I guess," I say quietly.

I told him yesterday it was just a basic introductory appointment. I was able to get all my medical records transferred to Dr. Sanderson's office, so they'll only be having me fill out paperwork, take some basic measurements, and listen to the baby's heartbeat today.

I don't see why he'd *want* to come to any of that.

We get to the hospital, and Duke navigates around the small maze of offices behind it. We walk in the front door and the receptionist greets us with a warm welcome. She certainly seems to know Duke, but he doesn't look in her direction. She hands me a clipboard to fill out, and we take a seat in the waiting room.

Everything is straightforward until I get to the portion about the biological father, requesting their information as well. *Crap.* Should I fill it out? Does it matter? I don't want to put *his* name down on *anything* pertaining to my baby. I don't even want to *speak* his name...

"Maci?" Duke whispers, placing a hand on mine to steady the shake.

I look away, roughly swiping at the falling tears. "I'm fine."

He points to a small box off to the side near the father's section that states: *N/A – Not applicable.* I nod solemnly, checking the box.

A nurse calls my name, and I stand.

"I'll, um, wait here for you," Duke grunts.

"You can come with me if you want," I say.

He takes in a deep breath, his leg jumping. "You sure?"

I can hear it in his tone—he *wants* to.

I nod. He walks with me as we follow the nurse into a room. Duke takes a seat in the guest chair, holding my coat and purse for me. The nurse checks my blood pressure and weight before handing me a urine cup. She instructs me to use the bathroom down the hall.

Finishing my business, I return to the room where Duke is waiting. His stern expression locked on a poster of a realistically drawn vagina with the head of a baby crowning from a side view—cutting the mother in half to see the birthing process from the inside.

I snicker, closing the door behind me. "Learn anything?" I tease, hopping to sit on the exam table with a loud crinkle of that obnoxious paper under my butt.

He scoffs. "Yeah, ten centimeters is a lot."

I burst with laughter at the same time a knock hits the door. In walks a kind-eyed, older woman with silver-blonde hair. Her eyes shine as she looks at me. "Hello, Miss Baker. My name is Dr. Clara Sanderson. It's lovely to meet you." She extends her hand to me and I take it.

"It's nice to meet you, too," I say as her attention turns to Duke with surprise.

"Duke Montgomery," she announces. "Your brother was just in here with his fiancée not even a week ago. Julie didn't tell me I'd be seeing you as well."

His tone is tight as he says, "Hi, Mrs. Sanderson."

Duke and his family know my new OBGYN on a personal basis?

How small *is* this town?

Dr. Sanderson waves him off, taking a seat on the rolling chair and turning to me. She grabs the clipboard I filled out, flipping through to the *father's information page*, and it's written on her face as she glances between Duke and me.

She clears her throat and grabs a pen, going through my information and making notes where she sees fit. Until she gets to that dreaded portion again. "I see here you've marked not applicable for the father of the child." Her kind eyes lift to me. "Do you have any medical history or information on the father that you'd like us to make note of?"

I peer at Duke out of the corner of my eye. "There's a...history of high blood pressure on the biological father's side. But that's all I'm aware of."

Dr. Sanderson jots down the note. "I take it you'll be raising this child on your own?"

"Yes, ma'am," I say with as much confidence as I can muster, but it's not much.

She smiles, standing and setting the clipboard on the counter. "Good for you," she says with a fire in her eyes that tells me she means every word of it. "Now, lay back for me, dear, and let's get a quick measurement."

I lay back and pull my shirt up under my breast, the pop of my belly even more prominent in this position. Dr. Sanderson does some feeling around my belly and lower pelvis. "I understand you're new to town. I'd recommend you set up a tour of the hospital here in Whitetail, and the birthing center in Deerhide. I deliver at both, wherever you decide to go is completely up to you. But I will say, if you're interested in a water birth, the birthing center is the only spot set up for it."

"Water birth?" Duke repeats, horrified.

Dr. Sanderson laughs. "Yes, Duke. Your mother delivered three of you Montgomery boys during a water birth. This was back when the hospital was set up for it, however. I think you and Butch were water births, if I remember correctly."

"You delivered Duke?" I ask in awe.

Dr. Sanderson smiles wide. "Oh, yes, dear. Julie Montgomery and I go way back. I've been delivering babies in this town for over forty years. That includes all six of the Montgomery siblings, and apparently, the grandbabies, too."

We go over a few more things, like my ideal birth plan—which is an epidural. A very, *very* strong epidural. Dr. Sanderson takes my measurements, then pulls out a fetal heart monitor from her white coat pocket.

I glance at Duke watching every move Dr. Sanderson is making with a stern expression.

"Let's get a listen to this little one," she quips, placing the small, cool wand on my belly with a firm press.

Muffled movement is all we hear at first, and then—the signature fast beat of a tiny heart. I cover my mouth, feeling the floodgates ready to pour.

"And that...is your baby's heartbeat. A strong 160. Absolutely perfect," she tells me, letting us listen for another moment before she pulls away, offering a hand to help me sit up.

Dr. Sanderson smiles softly as she hands me a tissue. "You're all set today, Maci. Please make sure to stop at reception to schedule your next appointment. Keep doing what you're doing, and we'll see you in another four weeks."

I dab under my eyes and sniffle. "Thank you, Dr. Sanderson."

The second she closes the door, I sob, hiding my face in my hands as strong arms wrap around me. I bury my face into Duke's broad chest, holding onto him as hard as I can. He doesn't say a word, simply holds me tight while I continue to cry.

It's been a hard, stressful few months and...something about *hearing* the reason for it all makes everything worth it.

I finally reel it in enough to release my death grip on Duke. He grabs the box of tissues off the counter and silently offers them to me.

I take a few, then slide off the exam table. "Thanks," I sniffle, my gaze rising to Duke's whose eyes are a little bloodshot themselves. My lower lip wobbles at the very thought of him crying too, but he just grins.

We don't say anything walking to reception. I schedule my next appointment before we head out to Duke's truck. He helps me in, and says, "You know what, I think I left my phone in there. I'll be right back." He closes the door before I have a chance to say anything.

I watch him jog across the parking lot back into the office. He's gone for roughly five minutes, and I wonder if he got held up talking to Dr. Sanderson—or that perky receptionist.

I mean, not that I *care*. Well, I do. Sort of...

He did say we're *exclusive*. We agreed not to have sex with other people. Does that mean he could *date* other women so long as he doesn't have sex with them? But I've been with him non-stop for three weeks—he wouldn't, would he?

I shake my head, desperate to get rid of the thought as he comes out of the office stuffing a white envelope in his coat pocket. *That's...strange.*

"Hungry?" he asks, starting the engine.

I sigh. "Yes."

"Good." He gives me a lopsided grin and a wink, driving in the direction of the town diner. I can't help but smile when he takes my hand once again. When he brings the back of it to his lips, kissing it softly, I nearly break down.

It's a small gesture, one that makes keeping him at arm's length from my heart harder and harder by the second.

Sixteen.

Maci

"GREAT JOB EVERYONE." I smile, standing from my yoga mat. I give a quick goodbye to the seven couples leaving the mirror-lined studio in the private gym at Winton's Ski Resort & Mountain Spa.

Waiting for the next class to arrive, I busy myself by wiping down the mats for the final class of the day. The one where Cassidy is bringing Butch, Alison is bringing Tanner, and Stan is bringing some lady friend I can't remember the name of.

What I don't anticipate is Duke to be the first one walking through the door. His dark eyes drink me in from head to toe in my high-waisted, fitted black yoga pants and matching sports bra. It leaves a good portion of my midriff showing.

"Goddamn, doll," he growls, his steps longer as he approaches with a wicked grin.

I jump back, but he's too quick. He snatches my waist and lays a hot and heavy kiss right on my lips. His large palms squeeze my ass in a punishing grip. I smile against his lips. "What are you doing here?"

"I came to watch the show," he jokes. "You couldn't pay me not to be here to watch Butch do fuckin' yoga."

I snort. "You're horrible."

He chuckles deeply, smacking my ass playfully. "Why haven't I seen you in these pants before? Fuckin' hell, your ass in these…"

I smile so wide it hurts my cheeks. Always with the compliments, this one. Another reason why he's now classified as *one-in-a-million*. "Because these are fitted for yoga. And they're quite expensive, so don't mess with them."

He pouts, giving my ass one last rough fondle. "I'll buy you a dozen more to wear around the cabin every day."

I swat his chest playfully. "Okay, okay, stop that. Everyone should be here soon."

"Yes, ma'am," he says, kissing me sweetly.

Alison and Tanner are the first to arrive. Stan arrives next, introducing a thin blonde named Beverly. When Butch and Cassidy walk in, however, they're not alone.

Duke bursts with laughter. "Ma. Pop. What the hell are you doing here?"

Butch scowls, gesturing to his fiancée. "She invited them."

"Sorry, I hope that's okay," Cassidy adds. "I know you said the class wasn't full, so I figured…"

I wave her off. "Absolutely."

Duke's mother is a petite blonde with stunning pale blue eyes—and for having six kids, she's in amazing shape—appearing to be in her late fifties. His father is big, easily six-foot-four, broad like his sons, and clearly in his later sixties, early seventies.

But the way they're holding hands...it's giving me all the feels.

"You must be Maci Baker," Duke's mother beams, giving me a tight squeeze. "I have heard so much about you. I'm Julie. This is my husband, Clayton. We're so happy to finally put a face to the name. And a beautiful one it is."

I blush. "Thank you, Mrs. Montgomery."

"No, no, dear." She waves her finger sternly. "It's Julie and Clayton. We're young, hip, and happening."

Cassidy giggles. "That's right, Mama Jules."

Butch and Duke groan.

"Good to meet ya, Maci." Clayton shakes my hand in a firm hold. "So, tell me, what are we in for?"

"Couple's Yoga." I smile. "Or better known as Tantric Yoga."

"Tantric," Clayton repeats in confusion. "Isn't that the sex stuff?"

"What?" Butch barks out, horrified as he swivels on Cass. "You invited my parents to *sex* yoga!"

Julie scowls at her eldest son. "Knock it off, Butch Robert Montgomery. You sit down and listen to what Miss Maci has to teach us."

I cover my mouth to muffle my laughter as Duke bites his cheek, grinning. He must love watching his brother still get in trouble at his age.

"It's not *sex* yoga," I correct him. "What I teach is a milder version of tantra, suited for any couple. Beginner or advanced. Whether you've been together for a few days or a few decades, I'm going to help you align yourselves with one another on a more sensual and spiritual level."

"I think we got this, honey." Clayton wraps his arm around his wife. "Let's show these kids how they were made."

Everyone bursts with laughter, except for Duke and Butch who look mortified.

I go to the front of the studio to stand on my mat. "If everyone could take a mat with their partner and remove your shoes—socks optional. We can get started."

"Ah, shit," Stan mutters. "Keep your boots on Butch, you'll smoke us all out."

There are a few snickers around the room as everyone picks a spot. All the ladies are dressed in proper yoga gear. While the men have on a sea of random workout gear, all suitable. Even Duke showed up in a pair of his more relaxed pants.

I wonder...

"Why's Duke in the back?" Butch grunts, glaring over his shoulder.

"I'm observing." Duke grins, snapping a picture of the unruly student.

"The fuck you are," his brother says, gesturing to the front. "Get up there."

"Do you normally teach alone, Maci?" Julie asks.

I bite my lip with a smile. "I do, but you know what... Duke, would you mind helping me out this evening?"

His smile fades instantly, the blood draining from his face.

Butch chuckles darkly.

"Come on now, dear, you're holding up the class," Julie scolds.

Duke grits his teeth, kicking off his shoes in the back of the room, and tossing his hoodie to the side. He strides to me with a glare. I smile, hitting play on the calming playlist over the Bluetooth speakers as I dim the lights. "Let's start with some simple stretches to loosen up," I announce, instructing everyone accordingly.

We go through a few stretches as well as a few solo yoga poses to give everyone a feel for what we'll be doing with our breathing. "Now, I'd like everyone to sit back-to-back with their partner, legs crossed, knees angled out. Align your hips, your spine, shoulders—as best you can with any height difference."

Butch leans back to kiss Cassidy, his sour demeanor diminishing once he gives her his full attention.

"Resting your hands on your knees, I want you to inhale a deep breath through your nose, and bring your shoulders up with your partner. Exhale *with* your partner. Inhale slowly, exhale. Let's do several more of these breaths. Be sure to *feel* the breath you're taking with your partner."

Duke and I align and begin our breaths. He brings his hand around, gripping the side of my ass out of sight for everyone. *Tease.* I swat his hand.

"Inhaling, extend your arms up above your head," I say. "Now exhaling, we're going to let our arms fall to the side and twist to our right. Your right hand is going to touch your partner's left knee, and your left hand is going to rest on your right knee. Press with your inhale, and *feel* that stretch of your spine. Exhale, pull to deepen if you can.

"Hold for a moment," I add. "Release back on exhale with your partner, twisting now to the left. Use your partner to feel that stretch, go as deep as you can, inhaling deep, exhaling slow. Beautiful, everyone.

"And release. Perfect." I smile. "Now we're going to bring our feet together in front of us, bring them as close to your groin as you can. You don't have to go extreme, whatever is comfortable to you.

"Now we're going to lean. I'm going to lean forward first—if you'll watch me. I'm going to have Duke lean back against me, extending his arms out. Keeping our spines aligned, we're going to lean together as one," I say, leaning forward.

"Duke, let your head fall between my shoulders," I instruct. "It's important to communicate with your partner, so I'm going to have Duke apply more pressure to me so I can go deeper into the stretch. So, Duke, lift your hips, lean back, and press into me. Continuing to inhale with your partner, exhale. Duke will rock his head slowly from side to side, giving me that pressure right at the top of my spine.

"Go ahead, start your lean, and just breathe together," I say as everyone takes the position.

"I feel like I'm hurting you," Duke whispers.

"You're not. It feels amazing." I sigh. "Communicate with your partner, let them tell you when they've had enough of the stretch before changing." I inhale deeply. "We're going to switch, so we'll release up on an exhale, and now I'm going to lean back into Duke as he leans forward. You'll see I need to press my feet into the mat because of the size difference. Adjust yourselves accordingly."

Leaning back into Duke, he groans.

"Deeper?" I ask.

"Yeah," he says, and I do. "Fuck. That does feel good."

Cassidy laughs. "Butch, babe, I can't push any harder."

"Christ," Clayton grunts. "You're gonna have to pick me up with a forklift after this one."

Duke snorts, and I bounce on his back with a laugh.

"Bring your hips down, feet together, spines aligned, and we're going to move into one of my favorite heart-opening exercises."

The class goes by smoothly. A few more jokes are thrown around, lightening the mood for everyone. Getting into the final resting pose. I instruct the ladies to sit between their partner's thighs, wrapping their legs around them. Foreheads pressed together, arms resting on each other's waist.

I check everyone's positions before sitting on Duke's lap. He wraps his arms around me, whispering, "If I get a boner in front of my parents, you're in deep shit."

I smile mischievously.

"Bring your partner in gently with each inhale. *Feel* their body become one with yours as you breathe through to fully relax in their embrace." I inhale deeply, eyes drifting closed. "Let your hands roam to your subconscious desires. Embrace the presence of your partner..."

Duke holds me tight, his breathing jagged as his large hand slides to my belly, resting over my bump.

I suck in a sharp breath, my eyes flying open to stare at him. His jaw locks tight, and I shake my head lightly against his. *Don't do this. Not now.* I pull away to see if anyone is watching us, and thankfully, no one is.

"Maci, I..." he whispers, nearly inaudible.

I clear my throat and remain seated between his thighs. "And that's it," I say. "You've all just completed your first class in couple's yoga."

Julie claps. "I loved it."

"That was great, Maci," Alison praises.

"What'd you think, babe?" Cassidy asks Butch.

"It was all right," he grunts, distracted as his hands continue to roam her ass.

"Woah there, tiger." Stan laughs. "Your parents are right there."

"Can you show us something harder?" Tanner asks. "What do you do with the advanced couples?"

"Oh, yeah, show us," Alison beams.

I look to Duke. "Can you hold my entire body weight without dropping me?"

He scoffs. "Yeah."

Standing, I adjust my pants higher. "Okay, but I don't recommend doing this unless you completely trust your partner. You can get seriously injured if you try this without proper stretching and strength."

Duke's eyes widen. "What?"

"Relax," I say. "Lay on your back, shoulders flat, legs up in a squat, feet together." He reluctantly gets into position. I sit on his feet facing away from him, glancing over my shoulder and down at him. "Put your arms up straight, palms flat. You're going to push me up with your feet until your legs are straight."

"But—"

"Just hold firm, and I'll do the rest," I say calmly. "I trust you. Do you trust me?"

He huffs out an exaggerated breath, eyeing me warily. "Yes."

I nod, and he pushes me up with his feet. I bend, letting my shoulders fall into his palms. "Bend your elbows." He does, and I kick my legs up so only the top of my butt rests on the very tips of his feet. I extend one leg, bend the other, and point my toes. Arms extended to the side, I throw my head back and come face to face with Duke while hanging upside down.

His gaze never leaves mine, and for a moment, I'm suspended in time. The two of us. Here. Now. I take a deep breath and know he's doing the same. We're in sync, him and I. Two souls connected by a thread of pure trust.

"Holy shit."

"We are *not* trying that, Tanner."

"Now bring your legs to bend slow, and push my shoulders up with your arms," I tell Duke. I'm back on my feet a moment later to the sound of applause.

"That was like...some fancy trust fall." Cassidy turns to Butch.

"No."

A breathy laugh escapes me. "Like I said, it takes a lot of core strength and trust to do some of the more difficult poses. But thank you for coming tonight. I hope you all enjoyed your time and feel a little more connected."

"I feel connected to this mat," Clayton grumbles. "Butch, help your old man up."

Butch and Duke each grab a hand to hoist their father to his feet. I say goodbye to everyone on their way out, while Butch and Cassidy linger.

Duke helps me wipe down the mats and roll them up for the night.

"Thank you."

"For what?" he asks. "Helping you clean up or for forcing me to join the class?"

"Both." I smile. "What'd you think, though? Did you like it?"

"Yeah, my back feels amazing," he says. "But I'm not gonna lie, you scared me with that last one. I knew I wouldn't drop you, but you didn't need to tell me if I fucked up, you'd get hurt."

I put on my socks and boots. "You needed to be aware of the posing danger. Advanced is called advanced for a reason. I've only ever done that pose with other instructors, never a newbie."

"Is that supposed to make me feel better?"

"You did great. That pose was perfect. I can't wait to see the picture someone took."

"That was me," Cassidy sings, waving her phone in the air.

Duke pulls on his shoes and hoodie, grabbing my coat and purse for me while I tug on my lavender sweater, and take the phone. The picture is stunning. My favorite part might be how cute my bump looks—and the big smile on Duke's face.

Butch tips his head to his brother. "Did Ma talk to you about the cabin yet?"

"No," Duke says warily. "What is it now?"

Butch scratches his beard, glancing over at me before he says, "Beau's rentals have been getting a lot of attention for bookings with all the snow on the mountain this season. And, uh, he went ahead and opened the availability online before checking with Ma."

"Shit," Duke hisses. "Did she call him?"

"Oh yeah, but you know how Beau is. And Ma can't ever say no to him, so she was hoping...you'd be willing to move back home for a bit while you wait on the build, or until the bookings slow in the spring."

Panic seizes my chest. Do they not know I've been living there, too?

"Hell no," Duke responds immediately.

"I figured you'd say that," Butch says. "We talked about it, you're welcome to crash at our place for the time being. Cass already picked which room is the baby's, so the spare room is open for you."

Duke rubs his face roughly. "Can't Ma cancel the bookings?"

"Pop told her to, but..."

"Beau," Duke mutters, not meeting my terrified stare.

"Where did you live before the cabin?" I ask quietly.

"Owned a house in town," he says. "Sold faster than I anticipated. And I wasn't going to sign a lease for a year when I knew I'd end up breaking it."

Cassidy looks between Duke and me. "You could always room with Maci when she finds a place. You'll need two bedrooms anyway for the baby. I'm sure the extra rent money would help."

I fight down a cringe. She has no idea I've been staying with him for weeks.

Butch's brow furrows. "Where are you staying?"

Biting my lip nervously, I stare up at Duke. He's deep in thought; jaw ticking, eyes dark. I clear my throat that feels like it's closing shut. "Um..."

Cassidy beams, completely unaware of how devastated I'm feeling at this moment. *So much for that string of bad luck ending…*

"Do you know any places for rent, babe?"

Butch's gaze remains on me, ignoring his future wife and scowling with an intensity that screams he *knows*, and he's judging me. "No. Places for rent are scarce right now. Remember when you tried to find a place? It was next to impossible. Nothing is going to be available until spring, guaranteed."

My stomach does a stress-induced flip. I hold a hand over my belly and take in a deep breath, trying to push the upset nausea feeling down. *Breathe, Maci. Breathe.*

Duke rests a hand on my lower back. "Ah, fuck. Come on, Maci," he says, taking my hand and wrapping an arm around me as he urges me out of the studio. "Hold on, angel, the bathroom's right over here."

I let him take control. Trusting him…

It's then, I realize, I'll never have anyone read me better than he does.

Seventeen.

Duke

"I'm okay," Maci says, wiping her mouth with a paper towel. "I just need a minute."

I reach for the door handle to the restroom. "I'll be right outside, okay?"

She nods, sniffling.

I don't want to leave her alone and upset, but if she needs a moment, I'll give it to her. I walk out toward the studio where my brother stands waiting.

"Is she okay?" Cassidy asks when I approach.

I keep a watchful eye over my shoulder for any signs Maci might need me. "Yeah, she's okay." I sigh. "She gets nauseous when she's upset. And with the pregnancy...she tends to get sick easily."

Butch eyes me sternly. "She's living with you at the cabin, isn't she?"

I don't respond.

"What the hell are you thinking, man? You hardly know this woman," he barks.

My jaw tightens. "You don't know what you're talking about."

For a split second, my brother's expression softens. That damn look. The one I've been forced to be on the receiving end of for years now. And I loathe it more than anything.

"You know she's not—" he starts.

I'm in his face a split second later. "If you know what's good for you, you won't finish that sentence," I threaten, gritting my teeth. "I know who she is, and I know what I want. For the last time, our relationship is *none* of your business. So, back. The fuck. Off."

Cassidy steps between us. "Stop it. Both of you. Maci is already upset. She doesn't need to come out here and hear you two fighting again. She's here, she's pregnant, and she's staying. Even if we need to offer her a place to stay, too."

Butch snaps his head to Cassidy, and his glare says it all.

"Don't worry about us," I seethe. "I've got it handled."

Butch scoffs. "Then you should know the cabin is booked for the twenty-third."

That's two days away. *Shit.*

I bite my tongue when Maci finally emerges from the restroom and toes her way to my side. Her face is pale, eyes bloodshot, and nose bright red. "Sorry about that," she says quietly.

I want to tell her she has nothing to apologize for, but think better of it given our current audience. "Ready?" I ask.

She nods, turning off the studio lights and locking the door.

My brother follows our lead with his fiancée tucked at his side, but I can't be bothered by their presence. I'm already weighing my—no, *our* options. Maci doesn't need this kind of stress. I just got her to draw back on the apartment hunt, now here she is throwing up because of it.

Unfortunately, places for rent *are* scarce. It's why I've been staying at the cabin.

When we reach the resort entrance Butch grunts, "Wait."

We stop while Maci digs through her purse for her keys.

"You think you'll be able to find something in two days?" Butch asks me.

"Two days," Maci whispers for only me to hear.

If he makes her throw up again, I swear...

"I've got it under control," I grind out, hoping the look I'm giving him explains the rest.

He sighs heavily, gazing down at Cass holding his arm with pleading eyes. "You're both welcome to stay with us until you find something or when your house is done."

I don't get a chance to refuse their offer because my future wife is too busy walking away from me. "It was good seeing you guys." She waves over her shoulder, tears streaming down her face as she forces a smile. "I'll see you Monday, Cassidy."

I follow her. "Maci," I call, picking up the pace to a near jog as she hustles through the parking lot. "Maci, wait." I reach out and catch her arm. "Babe..."

She whimpers, a cry in her voice. "What?"

I lift her chin to meet my gaze, swiping perfect tears from her flushed cheeks. "I'll make a few calls, doll. You don't need to worry. I'll take care of this for us."

She shakes her head. "There is no *us*, Duke, remember? We're friends with benefits. And you know what? You should find someone else. I'm not into whatever *wanna-be* relationship game you've picked me out for. Stay with your brother, I'll figure something out."

My chest tightens. Is that what she thinks? This is some fucking game? My hold tightens. "You don't mean that, angel. Let's get home and talk—"

"Yes, I do," she sobs. "Let me go, Duke, you're hurting me."

No. This is all wrong.

I release her only to stand there and watch her leave—torn between giving her space and chasing after her like a lovesick fool. I shake my head of the words she said. I know my girl. She didn't mean them. She's stressed and scared and I'm going to fix this.

I pull out my phone and jog to my truck to make a phone call to the brother stationed overseas. No one other than Ma has heard from him in almost a year, not that he minds. He's never had a caring bone in his body—he's always been *strictly* business.

And when the phone rings instead of going straight to voicemail, I thank every lucky penny I've ever picked up that he's got service wherever the hell he is.

"Duke," Beau rumbles. His voice grits like sandpaper on unpolished granite, and I'm surprised to hear he's lost his accent.

"Hey, brother."

ele

I arrive at the cabin a half hour later than Maci. I aimed to give her an hour's worth of space, but...well, here I am. All the lights are out, but I know she's here. Her car is parked out front, and the bedroom door is closed.

I knock lightly before pushing it open. "Maci?"

The light under the new bathroom door illuminates my path. I open the door only to reveal her shaking and sobbing on the floor. My heart aches to see her like this.

I drop beside her and gently coax her into my arms. She doesn't fight me as I bring her to rest on my chest, rubbing her back soothingly. "I worked it out with Beau," I say. "We can stay here, sign a lease, and pay a monthly rent. He even said this works better for him since he wants a regular tenant in this cabin. The bigger cabin next door is the one everyone wants for family vacations—not this one. We'll put your name on the lease, and it'll be all yours after that, all right? My house will be done in another four months, give or take. And if you'll let me, I'd like to stay here with you so I don't have to sleep on the twin-size bed from my childhood."

She lifts her head from my chest. "R-Really?" she chokes out, wiping her damp, quivering lips.

I brush the hair back from her face. "It's Beau's call. This is his property."

"Does he know I live here with you?" she asks quietly.

"He does now." And after the ass-chewing I tossed his way, he won't forget it.

Ma might have a hard time putting her black sheep, middle son in his place, but I sure as hell don't.

Maci throws herself at me, hugging me tight with a heartbreaking sob that hits me deep. I hold her close as she hides her face in my neck. "I'm sorry I snapped at you," she cries. "I-I didn't mean it. I really didn't. I'm so sorry, Duke."

I shush her cries as I hold her like this for a long moment until she finally lets me look at her. "Let's get you cleaned up." I help her in the shower and leave her to get ready for bed.

I sit on the couch in just my boxers and watch the fire I lit dance in front of me. Absently wondering how I'm going to get this out. I can't let her slip through my fingers.

The thought alone is too painful.

I glance at the bedroom door to find her standing there. Cautiously, she walks to me. Her hair is damp and pulled to one side, no makeup, and wearing one of my T-shirts that goes well past her ass.

When she gets within arms' reach, I bring her to straddle my lap. She hiccups, snaking her arms around my neck as she settles in. Her emerald eyes still red and puffy.

I take a deep breath. *Here goes nothing...*

I rub her thighs, leaning my head back against the couch. "We need to talk."

Her lower lip wobbles. "No."

I chuckle. "Yes, angel."

Her glossy eyes shine. "You're still going to call me that?"

"If you'll let me," I say with a heavy sigh. "I...like you, Maci. A lot. I don't want to play this *game*, as you called it. I want to be with you. *Us*. You and me. Not just some...feeling when we're alone."

Her hands drop from my neck to rest on my chest like she's bracing herself. "No, you don't," she whispers.

"I do." I gently lift her chin to face me. "And I need you to tell me how you feel."

She blows out a shaky breath. "I'm pregnant, Duke."

I nod, encouraging her to continue.

"It's not fair to you the...situation I'm in right now."

"I'm not asking for facts here, sweetheart," I say. "Tell me how you *feel*."

She shakes her head, on the verge of tears once again.

"Maci, I'm not going to sit here and act like I don't care that you're pregnant with another man's child, because I do," I grunt, and her face falls. I grip her hips to keep her from leaving. We need to get this out in the open. "I get that it's not fair. To you. To me.

But I don't care. We'll make it fair. For us, for the baby. I care about you, Maci. I care about your baby. I want you how you are. Even when you're sneaking out of bed at 2:00 AM to eat a spoonful of peanut butter."

"I knew you were awake," she says with a watery laugh.

I grin. "I meant it when I said I'm here for you. Now I'm here, wanting *both* of you. So, tell me, what do *you* want? Because I'll give you both the world if you'll let me."

Her lips part in a pretty gasp. "Oh, Duke."

"Be honest with me. I need to know."

A single tear escapes her. "I...I'm falling in love with you," she confesses, and my heart hammers in my chest. *God, yes.* "But...everything isn't going to be sunshine and sex six months from now. You won't be my first priority if we're together. You'll come second, maybe even third to other responsibilities. I can't ask you to take this chance on us. We'll both just end up getting hurt."

My jaw tightens. "You don't know any of that, Maci. And I have no problem coming second to the baby. I'd expect nothing less. You think I haven't thought it through a thousand times over? Because I have. It's all I've been able to think about since I met you. *You* have been my priority for the last three weeks, Maci. Both of you have."

"Duke—"

"I wish I would've met you before, doll, I do. But I wouldn't trade this life growing inside of you for anything." I place my hand over her stomach. "This baby is you. Beautiful, smart, peanut butter obsessed." She pains a smile, tears falling. "No, it's not always going to be sunshine and sex. Not now, not over the next six months, not for the rest of our lives if we're lucky. But don't think for a second, I won't be right there with you waking up in the middle of the night doing anything you ask of me for the two of you."

She starts to cry, and I hold her face in my hands. "If you don't want this, if you don't want me... Fuck. You better tell me now because I don't know if I'll ever let you go after tonight."

Her lips fall against mine with a hunger that fuels my own—it's an answer, a prayer, a damn Hail Mary to my soul. I kiss her back, tangling my hands into her long, damp hair. Her hands drop to my boxers, fumbling to slip past the elastic band and release my thickening cock.

Not wasting the moment, I tug my shirt up and over her head, tossing it to the side, and groan. *No panties.* Straddling me—emotions and body bare—I kiss her hard. The need to claim her, to finalize *us* has been building inside of me for weeks.

I cup her hot, greedy pussy and grind the heel of my palm against her clit. She moans into my mouth, stroking my freed length pulsing with need.

I rub my fingers through her silken folds, spreading the moisture from her sweet little hole. She positions herself over me, and before I have a chance to say otherwise, she drops her hips—impaling her tight cunt on my cock.

"Fuck," I groan.

She leans forward, bracing her hands on the back of the couch as she starts to move. Her breasts bounce in my face, tempting me for a taste. I suck one perfect pink tip into my mouth and guide her hips to move faster.

She moans. Her inner walls tighten around my length with every fall of her hips. And every second I'm drawn in closer—to release, to everything I've ever wanted.

Her forehead rests against mine. "Duke..." Her voice a husky, feminine plea.

Begging me.

Needing *me*...

"I'm gonna make you the happiest woman in the fuckin' world, angel," I growl, taking over her steady ride with a buck of my hips. My cock slams hard into her, and her legs tremble against my thighs.

"Yes," she cries.

I grip her ass, wrap an arm around her, lift her, and fuck her from below. She cups my face, our tongues twisting and turning as my thrusts pick up to a brutal pace. Fucking her deep, and making her *mine*.

Our combined release crashes into us at the same moment. She lets out a sexy-as-sin moan as her walls pulse and draw my cock deeper. The orgasm that rips through me has me pinning her above me with a jerk of my hips and a growl that's borderline feral. The punishing grip I have on her is sure to leave a mark in the morning.

With my claim coating the inside of her trembling pussy, my pounding heart beating in time with hers, and our panting breaths mirroring one another—I've never felt more grounded.

I hold her close as we come down from the high, knowing this time was different. We're not faking this anymore. This isn't a game. This is *real*—us.

The *three* of us.

And I'll do everything in my power to keep it that way.

Eighteen.

Duke

"Duke, wake up. There's someone at the door."

My eyes snap open at the sound of her honey-sweet voice. My arm is wrapped around her, keeping our naked bodies pinned against one another, and our legs intertwined.

I groan, hauling her flush to my chest to cuddle and go back to sleep.

A loud bang hits the sturdy oak of the front door, echoing throughout the cabin.

"Go see who it is." Maci yawns, sliding deeper under the blanket.

I huff in annoyance. "It's Sunday. Fuck 'em."

The banging continues.

I sigh loudly with a bit of an aggressive edge to it that earns me a soft peck on the cheek. "Fine," I grunt, keeping her covered as I get out of bed and walk to the bedroom door.

"Put some pants on first, babe." She giggles.

I stop and stare down at my half-chub of morning wood, and grumble under my breath. I grab a pair of sweats and yank them on. The commotion at the front door gets louder and more impatient. "I'm going to kill whoever the hell that is," I growl as Maci tries to hide her laughter under the covers.

I storm to the front door, unlock the deadbolt, and fling it open with more force than necessary. It takes a moment to register that it's my brother and his fiancée standing on the front porch. "What?"

Frankie, Cassidy's overweight redhaired dachshund, yips in greeting. His whole body wiggles in excitement when I stare down at him.

Butch looks at me strangely. "What are you wearing?"

I waste a glance at my only piece of clothing being black sweat pants with a huff in frustration. "If that's all you came here for, I'm seriously going to kick your ass."

Cassidy tips her head to the side. "What's on your nose?"

Oh. I reach up and peel off the nasal strip bridging my nose.

"Who is it?" Maci asks, coming out of the bedroom dressed in a pair of flannel pajama pants and *my* thermal long-sleeve. My heart and cock pulse in rhythm at the very sight of her.

This woman has no idea what she does to me...

Cassidy holds up two brown paper bags. "We brought a peace offering," she says, nudging my brother with her elbow. A cardboard tray containing four steaming drinks in his hands.

Frankie squeezes his thick waist between my leg and the doorframe. His nails click against the hardwoods as he scurries toward Maci cooing at his approach.

"You going to let us in?" Butch grunts.

"No," I deadpan, ready to slam the door shut and let Frankie stay when Maci slides in beside me.

She takes the door from me and opens it all the way. "Come on in," she says sweetly, like the angel she is.

I rake a hand through my disheveled hair with a sigh and move to the side.

Cassidy sets the bags down and starts removing a slew of muffins, bagels, and breakfast sandwiches. "I didn't know what you might be craving this morning, so we brought a whole bunch of stuff. Do you like butter or cream cheese on your bagels, Maci? I brought a side of both," she says, taking the tray of drinks from Butch who's attempting a heated stare-down with me.

Maci smiles, bringing four plates to the table and a water bowl for Frankie. "I've got this berry-flavored cream cheese. It's *so* good. Did you want to try it?"

"*Mmm*, absolutely," Cassidy beams, turning to Butch and me. "Come sit, Duke. Babe, remember what we talked about?" She raises a brow, crossing her arms in challenge to the giant dick in the room.

He grunts, taking a seat beside her.

I sit and lean back with my arm thrown over my girl's chair, tugging her close. My brother watches my actions with a stern expression and a lingering question in his eyes.

My only response is to boldly tilt her chin up. Maci meets my gaze with a small smile playing on her lush lips. Everyone else in the room disappears when my lips touch hers. I kiss her softly and fight down a weighted groan rising in my chest.

"I knew it." Cass claps, bouncing in her seat. "I told you. They *are* together."

My brother rubs his jaw, eyeing us as my arm drops around her waist and she leans into me. Cassidy places the coffee in front of Butch and me, while handing Maci her matching drink of a peppermint mocha—heavy on the whipped cream.

"Listen, Cass," I start, clearing my throat. "I appreciate you bringing breakfast, but what are y'all doing here?"

"It was either us or Ma," Butch says flatly.

Cass sips her drink. "We're here to apologize for yesterday. We didn't know you guys were living together. Julie feels awful about the whole thing. And we do, too. We should've been more sympathetic to the situation."

My brother scoffs, earning a glare from his fiancée.

"Y'all should feel like shit," I agree.

"Duke," Maci scolds, "It's not their fault they didn't know. We weren't exactly being open about what's going on between us."

Butch's brow furrows. "And what *is* goin' on between the two of you?"

Cassidy swats his arm. "We're not here to interrogate, remember? We're here to apologize and grovel for their forgiveness."

Maci laughs. "There's no need to grovel, Cassidy. It's totally fine. Apology accepted." Her all too forgiving, beautiful eyes meet mine. "Right, honey?"

My jaw tightens. The urge to say, '*No, make them grovel.*' lodges in my throat when she gives me that sweet, encouraging smile. I opt to kiss her instead, then turn to my future sister-in-law, currently carrying my niece or nephew and trying hard to keep my asshole brother reeled in. "Yeah, we're good."

Butch lifts his chin to me. "Sorry, man."

"Don't apologize to me. You're *my* brother. I don't have a choice but to deal with your bullshit," I say, looking at my future tucked under my arm. "Apologize to Maci."

Maci shakes her head. "No, it's—"

"I'm sorry for how I've acted these last few weeks," he tells her. "I've been less than welcoming to you, and I apologize for that."

Cassidy and I share a look, and she bites her lip with a smile.

Maci nods. "Thank you."

A beat later, Cassidy asks, "So *now* will you tell us what's going on with you two? Are you...?"

I grin from ear to ear, peering down to see Maci blush. "We're together."

"When did she move in?" Butch asks.

"Few weeks ago," I admit. "We made it official last night."

"I'm really happy for you guys," Cass adds, all giddy beside my stonewalled brother. "Julie is going to flip. She seriously thought Beau ruined whatever was happening between you two. Clayton had to hold her back from coming here—*literally*."

I scoff, knowing she isn't exaggerating in the slightest.

"I don't want to be the one to pry here..." Butch starts, eyeing me uncertainly.

Of course, he *does*. The bastard can't help but insert himself when it comes to me *finally* moving forward with my life.

Before I have a chance to tell him it can wait, Maci says, "It's fine."

His attention, and question, solely directed at her. "Have you talked this out? Not to state the obvious here, but you've got a kid on the way that ain't my brother's."

Cassidy throws her hands in the air, and I scowl right along with her.

"That's none of your—" I begin to say, my blood boiling, when Maci stops me with a raise of her delicate hand.

"They're family," she says. "He has a right to be worried about you."

Debatable, I seethe.

"We talked about it in depth, actually," Maci replies honestly. "We understand what we're getting into with starting this relationship now, but we owe it to each other to give this a try before the baby comes."

"I assume you know about Rachel?" he asks, and Maci nods. "Then you already know why I have concerns for my brother and this relationship."

"I do," she says, but...she doesn't.

I haven't told her that not only did I lose my wife, but our unborn child she was carrying. I'm just not sure...how to say it? How she'd feel about it? What difference it makes?

"There's nothing to worry about, Butch," I chime in, needing to deflect the direction of this conversation until I'm ready—and know how to handle it. "We're doing this aiming for the long haul."

Maci's eyes soften, and Cassidy bursts into tears. Frankie whimpers at her feet—whether that's because she's upset or looking for food, it's hard to say.

"Christ, Sunshine." Butch chuckles, wrapping an arm around her. "What the hell ya crying for? I thought you wanted them to be together."

Cass waves her hands at her eyes, blowing out a shuddering breath. "Well, y-yeah, but they're just so cute t-together."

Maci laughs, leaning into me. I hold her close and rub the side of her growing bump. A wave of happiness, joy, and purpose settles over me.

Everything is finally falling into place.

Nineteen.

Maci

"IF YOU DON'T FEEL good, we don't have to go," Duke tells me for the third time, standing in the doorway of the bedroom as I get ready.

He's just trying to get out of going himself.

I shimmy on the black stockings under the long-sleeved, olive-green sweater dress I borrowed from Cassidy. The form-hugging dress falls just below my knees and has my almost fourteen-week bump popping. I've done my hair, my makeup, and even brought out my grandmother's earrings. A little nausea and heartburn isn't going to stop me from enjoying a cookie decorating contest and dinner party at Duke's parents' for Christmas Eve.

I glance at him, a mouthwatering kind of handsome in his black slacks and dark grey dress shirt tucked in. Deep chestnut hair slicked back, his short beard shaped and trimmed exactly how I told him I liked it.

"I told you, I'm okay," I say, walking to the bathroom. "Cassidy said she bought peppermint hot chocolate. I'm sure once I get some of that in me, I'll feel better." I busy myself by checking my reflection in the mirror.

Duke appears behind me, grinning. "You look gorgeous, angel."

I pout, angling my backside toward him. "You don't think it makes my butt look too big?"

He chuckles deeply, wrapping strong arms around me. "I think it makes your ass look amazing, just like every other part of you."

I roll my eyes and smile. Always the charmer. "Thank you."

"But if you don't feel well, we can—"

I bump him back with my ass. "We're going. Your mom even called this morning to make sure we were coming tonight," I say. "I promise I'll tell you if I start to not feel well, okay?"

He huffs, peppering my neck with kisses. "You say the word, and we're out of there."

I bite my lip as he rubs his large hand gently over my belly, his dark gaze locked with mine in the mirror. I place my hands over his and lean into him. Three little words linger on the tip of my tongue. I've caught myself wishing—no, *wanting* to say them to him for days now.

Patience, I tell myself, *there's no rush*. He's made it clear he's not going anywhere.

"You ready to go, beautiful?"

I turn in his arms and kiss him. "Yes."

Duke takes my hand as I slide out of the truck. "Be careful. It's all ice right here." He keeps hold of me as he grabs the holiday poinsettia I picked out yesterday for his mom.

We make our slow way up the long driveway lined with vehicles to the classic white farmhouse equipped with several wreaths, garlands everywhere, and enough Christmas lights to signal outer space. And with the extra two feet of snow that's fallen over the last few days, it's going to be a magical white Christmas, indeed.

"Remind me again who's inside," I say, holding Duke's arm tight as my boots slip on the unsalted ice.

"My parents, Cass, you've met all my brothers except Beau, but he's not here. You'll meet my sister, Lily, and her son, Parker. My grandparents on my mother's side, William and Judy, and my Uncle Jim, Dad's brother," he says. "Looks like everyone is here except Rhett. Unless he rode with Levi."

When we reach the door, loud chatter and laughter echo from inside. As the door opens the smell of a holiday meal floods my senses—and makes me a little more nauseous, but I keep that to myself. The open archways off the foyer lead in every direction. A large dining table is set beautifully in the dining area to the right, while the living space is to the left where music plays. Traditional holiday décor lines three Christmas trees in view just from the front door.

This is how I want my baby to experience the holidays.

Duke takes my coat, hanging it up with his before leading me down the hall beside the wide staircase. I squeeze his hand, a little nervous to be officially introduced as his girlfriend—to his entire family—while pregnant.

I'm awestruck by the grand farm kitchen, lined with white cabinetry, butcher block countertops, a six-seater island in the center, and stainless-steel appliances throughout. Cassidy, Julie, and two other women help to set out appetizers.

"You're here," Julie announces, seeing us first. A Christmas-themed apron is wrapped around her waist covered in gingerbread men that says; *Nobody does holidays like Grandma.*

I nearly burst into tears at the sight. I'd blame it on the hormones, but...it's hard to deny the joy and acceptance I feel by simply walking in the front door.

Duke hugs his mother and hands her the poinsettia. "Oh, it's beautiful," she says. "Thank you so much, Maci."

I smile, hugging her. "You're welcome, but it's from both of us."

Julie pats her son on the arm, and winks. "Sure it is, dear."

After a quick greeting from Cassidy, who's wearing a matching dress to mine in red, she laughs when she tells us that Duke and Butch are dressed nearly identical.

Duke takes me around the house, introducing me to everyone I haven't met yet, and I can *feel* their eyes on my belly.

A handsome little boy with brown shaggy hair dressed in tan slacks and a collared flannel shirt barrels toward Duke. Cassidy's dog, Frankie, hot on his heels. "Uncle Duck!"

Duke snatches the boy, throwing him in the air to a slew of giggles. "Hey, bud, did you sneak any cookies yet?" He chuckles, wiping the smear of crumbs at the corner of the boy's lip.

"Nooo," he says with a mischievous smile, his pale blue eyes shining.

Duke turns to me with the boy perched on his forearm. "Parker, I want you to meet someone special." He grins. "This is my girlfriend, Maci. Can you say hi?"

"Hi, Parker." I wave. "How old are you?" He holds up three fingers, showing them proudly to me. "Woah. That's a lot."

Duke sets Parker down. "Hey, why don't you go sneak one of those peanut butter cookies with the chocolate kiss in the middle for Maci? She *loves* peanut butter."

Parker's eyes widen, and he wastes no time racing off toward the kitchen.

"You're going to get him in trouble," I tease.

"Nah, you haven't seen that kid sneak shit." He laughs. "He's a ninja."

"You make a good Uncle Duck."

He grins, dragging me flush against his warm, solid chest. "Just wait until you hear how he says Butch and Levi," he says, leaning down to kiss me.

A light tug on my dress has me looking down at Parker holding out a cookie for me. "Oh, wow. Thank you." I laugh, plucking the cookie from his small hand.

"Parker James," Julie shouts. "Did you take another cookie?"

Her grandson giggles and races off to the other room. And the night takes off from there. Duke stays by my side the whole evening. Whether it's a hand on my back, around my waist, on my thigh, or simply holding my hand in his—he's there.

And I'm drinking in every last second of his affection.

After dinner and cookie decorating, we take a seat in the living room, relaxing by the fireplace where all the stockings are hung. Multiple conversations go on around me, but all I seem to be able to focus on is the tiny red stocking pinned to Duke's with *my* name on it.

My stomach flutters.

"Maci?" Duke says, giving my thigh a rub.

"Yeah?"

"Lily asked when you're due."

"Oh, June thirtieth," I reply, sipping my mug of hot chocolate.

"Another June baby," Grandma Judy huffs, her tone rather cold.

"Aren't you due July eighteenth, Cassidy?" Lily asks.

"Yep." Cassidy smiles. "You never know, though. If Maci goes late, or I go early, we could be having them even closer together."

I scrunch my nose. "Hopefully not too late."

"I was early with all the boys," Julie chimes in. "You'll go early, Cassie-dear, trust me. These Montgomery boys grow fast and come out big."

Cassidy cringes while Butch grins far too wide at that news.

"The average birth weight of a child is generally somewhere between the size of the mother and father when they were born," Grandma Judy states matter-of-factly. "How large of a man is the father of your bastard, Maci?"

"Mother," Julie gasps, offended on my behalf.

The room falls deathly silent as all eyes turn to me.

I sink into the couch beside Duke, wanting nothing more than to crawl into a hole.

Duke's grip on my thigh tightens, but before he can say anything in my defense, his brother speaks first. "Keep your remarks to yourself, Gran," Butch threatens. "This ain't the fuckin' 1920s anymore."

Grandma Judy scoffs, crossing her arms, and sticking up her nose.

"Watch your tongue, boy," Grandpa William barks. "Bad enough you've knocked up your poor fiancée before you can make an honest woman out of her."

Butch's jaw locks tight, and if this were a cartoon, there'd be steam flying out of his ears.

Levi claps with a balk of laughter. "Rhett, get the popcorn!"

Rhett barrels into the living room with Parker on his shoulders. "Who's fighting this year? Should I get the mat?"

Uncle Jim swigs his whiskey with a laugh. "You two crotchety old fucks better watch out, these Montgomery boys will toss y'all out in the snow."

Clayton chuckles, but Julie glares at him, shutting him right up.

Unfortunately, that doesn't seem to stop Judy or William from continuing to comment on Butch and Cassidy's relationship, then Lily for having a child out of wedlock and moving back home to be supported by her parents.

The holidays, am I right?

Thankfully, my bladder gives me a reason to excuse myself. "Where's the bathroom?" I whisper to Duke. When he goes to stand, I stop him. "I'm not gonna be sick. I just need to use the bathroom."

He eyes me suspiciously. "You sure?" I nod and peck him on the lips. "Use the one upstairs. Down the hall, second door on the left."

I escape the most awkward after-dinner conversation I've ever been a part of and find the bathroom. I wash my hands and take my time walking back to the stairs when a wall of family pictures catches my eye.

I lean in to get a closer look. There are a few group pictures of when all the Montgomery siblings were young. It's hard to figure out who is who between some of the brothers, but boy were they cute chunky things when they were babies.

Going down the timeline of photos, around the teen years I start to notice a pretty, slender blonde in several photos with Duke. It's soon apparent who she is when I get to his wedding photo. *Rachel.*

She's in a short white summer dress, beaming on Duke's arm dressed in tan slacks and a white dress shirt. I narrow my eyes at the sand between their toes, appearing to be on a beach somewhere.

"We eloped on vacation," Duke says from behind, startling me to jump and turn to him.

"Sorry, I was just—"

"It's fine," he says, standing beside me. His dark eyes harden when he stares at the picture.

"She's very pretty," I say quietly.

"She was," he corrects.

Smooth, Maci. "How long were you two, um, together for?" I ask.

"We dated in high school on and off. Broke it off and went our separate ways for a good chunk of time. Found our way back to each other in the end. We were together for another three years before I asked her to marry me," he says. "I hate sand, but she always wanted to get married on the beach. So we did. We were married for about a year before the plane crash."

And that was five years ago... My heart sinks. "I'm sorry."

"Don't be." He turns away from the gallery of memories to face me. "It was a long time ago. I was a different person then."

"Was she your longest relationship?"

"Yeah, altogether was probably six years," he tells me. "What about you? How many *large men* have you dated?"

I snort. "Two years is my longest. And the only *large man* I've ever dated is *you*."

Duke cocks a smug grin as he steps closer, his muscular arms trapping me against him. "Good to know I can tear any of your exes apart if I need to."

I roll my eyes and pop up on my tippy toes to kiss him. "Your grandma is mean."

Duke grunts. "Yeah, well, you just missed the show. They're leaving now. Figured I'd come check on you."

"Aw, don't lie." I squeeze him. "You just missed me."

He grins from ear to ear, gripping my ass as he claims my lips in a hot and heavy kiss that has me clenching my thighs. I moan into his mouth, and he groans. "Fuckin' hell, angel. Tell me you're ready to get the hell out of here," he says, smacking my ass playfully.

I hum, pretending to think it over. "Can I have another slice of pie first?"

He chuckles. "The chocolate peanut butter pie?" I nod. "Anything you want, doll face," he says, taking my hand and leading the way to the kitchen.

"Drop that pie, Rhett," Duke demands as we cross the threshold.

Rhett freezes with a forkful of the last slice of chocolate peanut butter pie halfway to his mouth. "Why?" he asks a split second before Butch snatches the fork and plate from his hands. "Dude."

Rhett lunges for his plate, but Butch hands it straight to Duke. "What the fuck? I had it first."

"And now you don't," Duke deadpans, setting the plate on the island and pulling out the stool for me to sit.

I smile, hopping up on the stool. "We can share."

"No," Duke grunts.

Rhett snarls, grabbing a fork off the counter with a wicked grin on his face. He dives over the island in an attempt to stab the pie. Butch grabs him, and before I know what's happening, Levi is racing in—four Montgomery brothers in a wrestle on the kitchen floor over a slice of pie.

Cassidy sits calmly beside me with a lemon bar in hand.

"What the hell are you idiots doing?" Clayton booms.

"Duke stole my pie," Rhett exclaims from under a headlock while throwing an elbow back into Butch's gut.

Clayton just shakes his head, choosing a freshly frosted cookie off a nearby tray.

Julie snatches it from his hand. "You're already at your sugar limit for tonight, dear," she tells him, turning to her four wrestling adult sons. She sighs heavily. "Will you boys knock it off? Parker is getting tired, so we're going to do pjs now."

Duke drops Rhett like a sack of potatoes, jumping to his feet and rounding the island to stand behind me. "Touch her pie again, and you'll be shittin' sideways for a week."

Levi plucks the last lemon bar off the bake tray, and Butch promptly seizes his wrist. "Don't even think about it," he growls, and Cassidy quickly acquires the dessert from her soon-to-be husband.

"Seriously?" Levi says, exasperated. "So, no one is allowed to eat whatever the pregnant women want?"

Rhett mutters something under his breath about his favorite pie while watching as I shovel in an oversized bite of the delicious chocolate peanut butter bliss.

"Come on, kids," Julie calls from the living room, but I'm too invested in this pie at the moment.

Duke reaches for my plate, and I poke his hand with the fork. "No, sir."

He chuckles. "We'll bring it with us."

Heat rises to my cheeks, and I laugh. "Oh."

My pie plate in hand, we sit on the couch. Julie begins passing out gift bags. Handing the two largest bags to Butch and Duke, but the name on the side reads *Duke & Maci*.

She didn't...

Butch hands the bag to Cassidy. She pulls out a set of matching red flannel pajamas and a plaid, Christmas onesie for Frankie that says, *Nana is my favorite*. Duke opens his bag, removing a set of forest green flannel pajamas for—us?

"Did your mom buy us matching pajamas?" I whisper.

He simply grins. "And she's going to expect us to wear them tomorrow when we come over for Christmas brunch. It's mandatory. Along with the picture she's going to take of all of us together."

Oh, be still my heart. She's adorable.

"I hope you don't mind, Maci," Julie says. "I asked Duke your size. The bottoms should fit, but the top might be a little big. Last-minute holiday shopping is always a nightmare."

"Thank you so much, Julie, that's...really sweet of you." *Don't cry, don't cry.*

Parker starts to strip in the middle of the room to put on his new dinosaur pjs. Lily stops him, laughing. "Hold on, buckeroo. Give everyone a hug goodnight, and tell them we'll see them tomorrow when Santa comes."

Parker makes his rounds.

"Night, buddy. We'll see you in the morning," Duke says, giving him a bear hug. He crawls off Duke's lap and onto mine, throwing his little arms around me, and I melt.

"So, Uncle Butts, Jeans, and Duck," I say, crawling into bed. "I don't think I heard. What does Parker call Rhett?"

"Just Rhett," Duke replies, flicking off the lights and climbing into bed beside me. "He's only met Beau once in person, talked to him a few times on the phone, but he only knows him from pictures. Rhett and Beau are a lot easier for him to say."

I nod, snuggling up under the covers against his warm chest. "He's a sweet boy."

"He's a good kid. Shame his dad ran off the way he did."

"He's got five crazy uncles to look up to," I yawn. "I think he'll be all right."

"Yeah..." Duke sighs. "Do you, uh, ever worry about that? Raising a son or daughter without their real father?"

"Sometimes," I confess quietly. "I mean, anyone can be a father these days, but not everyone can be a *dad*. But I can do both. I've been working on my dad-joke game for many years now."

His chest rumbles under my cheek as he laughs. "Oh, yeah? Let's hear it."

I lift my head to look at him, resting my chin on the back of my hand. "Okay, but be prepared to pee yourself," I say, and he chuckles. "Why couldn't the bicycle stand up by itself?"

"Why?"

"It was *two-tired*." I giggle.

Duke groans. "Ah, babe, that was bad."

"It was not," I say defensively with a pout. "Fine. Let's hear you do a better dad joke."

"All right, give me a second," he says, forcing me to wait until he clears his throat. "I used to hate facial hair...but then it grew on me."

I burst with a laugh that causes me to snort.

"Boom, right there. Best dad-joke maker around, baby."

"That was awful," I tease, laying my head on his chest. "How'd I get so lucky?"

The question lingers openly in the air between us. And I do. I feel so, so lucky in this moment to have found him.

Duke pushes my legs open with his knee as he braces himself over me. Hovering just above my lips, he whispers deeply, "I'm the lucky one."

I slide my arms around his neck and kiss him with every ounce of my heart, because right now, it's all his.

Twenty.

Duke

I CARESS MACI'S BARE back as she lays naked on top of me, sleeping soundly. It's Christmas morning, and I know I need to wake her so we can get ready for brunch, but it's so hard to wake her when she's like this—beautiful, peaceful, all mine.

I kiss the top of her head, and glide my palms to her plump ass, grabbing a greedy handful.

"Stop it," she mumbles.

"Merry Christmas, angel," I rasp.

She yawns, nuzzling her face into my chest. "Merry Christmas, stud muffin."

I chuckle, causing her to bounce on my chest. Gently, I slide her to the side, and her adorable—albeit offended—pout has me grinning like a fool. "Don't look at me like that." I laugh. "I've gotta get something," I say, climbing out of bed.

She peeks over the covers, watching me leave the bedroom and come right back with a white envelope in hand that holds what I'm *hoping* was a good idea to get her for a Christmas present—back before I knew we'd be in a relationship.

Let's hope it's still good.

I sit on the edge of the bed and hand her the envelope. "Merry Christmas."

Maci sits up, holding the blanket at her chest in one hand and my gift in the other. "But..." She frowns. "I didn't get you anything."

"Good. Now, come on, open it."

Narrowing her eyes at me with a play of a smile, she opens the envelope. She takes the paper out and reads. And when her head snaps up to me with tears welling in her eyes, I know I did good.

"There's more," I say, signaling for her to flip to the other two pages. "It's a few days after you hit twenty weeks, but Dr. Sanderson said that's fine. You've got an appointment at *Hey, Baby – 3D/4D Ultrasounds* in Helena on Valentine's Day. It falls on a Friday, so I booked you a hotel for the weekend, and a pregnancy-friendly massage that Saturday. Everything is paid for, and I already talked to Peggy and the resort, so you're clear. I couldn't make dinner reservations this far out, but I'll make sure to call when the date gets closer."

"Duke, you—" She whimpers, tears streaming down her face as she throws herself at me.

I catch her easily and hold her tight against me, letting her have a moment before I ask, "Do you like it?"

"You're amazing," she cries softly, squeezing me.

I chuckle. "I'm glad you like it."

Pulling away, she wipes her eyes, glowing as she stares at the papers in her hand. "When did you do this? Is this why you went back into Dr. Sanderson's office after my appointment?"

"Yeah," I admit, rubbing the back of my neck. "I had Mandy help me find the ultrasound place. I didn't know what the hell I was looking for."

"The receptionist?"

My brow furrows. "Yeah, why?"

Maci shakes her head and laughs. "I thought you went back in there to hit on her."

"Mandy?" I balk. "Fuck no. We grew up together; she's like a sister to me. Although, I thought she was going to ruin the whole surprise with all that damn smiling she was doing."

"You did all this…" she trails off with a sniffle. "Before we even…"

"Made it official," I finish. "Yeah, I did. Hopefully, you're not too disappointed with not getting any diamonds or jewelry."

"Are you kidding me? This is the best present anyone has ever given me."

I give myself a mental high-five.

"You're coming with me, right?" she asks. "For the ultrasound and the weekend?"

My chest tightens. I want to go with her, but for her to *want* me to come with her—well, damn, she's giving me a gift in itself. "If you want me to." I force myself to play it cool.

"Of course, I do." She starts bouncing in place. "Ah! We get to find out the baby's gender on Valentine's Day," she squeals, jumping me and pinning me to the bed to shower me with kisses.

And in this moment with her, I don't know if I've ever been happier.

Ever.

The last seven weeks with Maci have been nothing short of a dream. She's everything I need, and everything I didn't know I desired in a partner. *I love her.* I love her more than I've ever loved anyone—I just can't bring myself to tell her.

There's no doubt in my mind she feels the same way, and I don't doubt she's waiting for me to say it first because of my past. And I'm working on getting to the point of telling her, I'm just not there yet.

Because the last time I spoke those three words to a woman I loved...

It was the last thing I ever said to her.

And that realization alone is messing with my mind.

Maci guides my hand onto her five-month bump, laying it flat against her. My heart warms feeling the tiny push under my palm.

That same heartwarming feeling I felt three weeks ago when we were in bed and she felt a kick for the first time.

The smiles, the laughs, the tears we shared.

Every second I spend with her is better than the last.

"They're moving all over the place," she says.

"Any final guesses?" I grin, rubbing her belly as I drive us to Helena for her ultrasound appointment and to enjoy a romantic weekend away—just us.

My family has welcomed Maci with open arms. We've gone to most of the Montgomery Sunday dinners when Maci is feeling well enough to go. And I refuse to go without her.

Butch and I are back on good terms ever since we made it official. He still has his concerns, but we've talked it out, and he understands I'm serious about this relationship—the baby included.

Maci places her hand over mine. "I'm sticking with a girl. What do you think? Cassidy keeps saying boy, but I think she's just saying that because she swears she's having a boy with how big she already is."

I chuckle. "Cass better hope it's a boy, I can't see Butch having a daughter. The guy will lose his mind."

"You think so?" She smiles. "I think it'd soften him up to have a girl."

"He'll be following her around like some lunatic by the teen years, guaranteed. And I'll be right there with him. The little lady born into the Montgomery's is going to have an escort for every dance, I'll tell ya that right now."

She laughs. "I can see it now."

We arrive at *Hey, Baby Ultrasounds* a minute later. The technician calls us back and into a private room. The space is clean, quiet, and dark. Maci gets on the bed, and the tech pulls up a chair for me to sit next to her. "My name is Katie; I'll be doing your ultrasound. Are we planning on finding out the gender today?"

Maci smiles. "Yes."

Katie squirts gel onto Maci's belly and presses against her with a white wand. "I'm going to start with a few measurements, then we'll take a closer look," she tells us, going through the necessary motions.

I glance over at Maci watching the screen with avid, rapt eyes. She takes my hand, and I squeeze hers in return. My nerves are shot, a jackhammer pounding in my chest. I haven't been this anxious since... Shit, ever.

"All right," Katie says. "Let's see what we're having..."

The wand twirls and shifts the view of the baby.

"It's a..." the tech pauses, anticipation rising, "...girl," she announces. "Congratulations."

A girl.

My heart swells.

Maci gasps, covers her mouth, and starts to cry. Hot tears sting my eyes as she reaches for me. She wraps her arms around my neck and holds me tight. "It's a girl," she cries softly.

I hold her, blowing out a jagged breath. "A girl." My voice strains with an overwhelming flood of emotion.

Maci leans away to look at me. Holding my face in her hands, she lays a tender kiss on my lips. "I love you, Duke," she whispers.

Time stops when she tells me she loves me. And I kiss her—again, and again, and again. *I love you, too*, I want to shout, but I don't. I...can't. Instead, I kiss her a hundred times to the point she's laughing tears of joy.

My whole life is right in front of me. "We're having a girl."

❧

"Close your eyes," Maci tells me, peeking out the bedroom door of the cabin.

I cross my arms over my chest and kick back on the couch where she told me to sit. "Why?"

She fakes a pout. "Please."

Reluctantly, I close my eyes and wait a beat before attempting to discreetly open one eye.

"Duke," she scolds me with a laugh.

I grin. She knows me too well. "All right, all right." I close my eyes and listen to her light steps as she approaches. I have a hunch as to what she's doing, but when I hear the rustle of paper, my brow furrows.

"Okay, you can open them now."

I open my eyes to Maci standing before me holding a large poster of a candy red, 1970 Chevrolet Chevelle SS 454 with the signature double black stripes on the hood—my dream classic muscle car.

"This is the one, right?" she asks with a beautiful smile.

I'm confused. "Yeah, doll, but why do you—"

"Good," she starts. "Because you're going to need this for reference when you go with Butch next week to pick up yours."

My mouth drops, my eyes widen, and I bolt to sit up straighter. "*What?* Are you—"

"It needs a lot of work," she adds, gazing down at the poster. "I know you mentioned you'd love to buy one to restore yourself. The guy said it doesn't run, and it might need a whole engine rebuild, but everything on it is original, including the red paint."

I stare at her in amazement. "Maci."

"Happy Birthday!"

"How?" I ask, completely dumbfounded.

"I've been looking for a while," she says. "Long story short, I found this guy in Colorado... He wanted the car to go to someone who would restore it and keep it as original as possible. I told him about you, and your whole plan—well, what I remembered you telling me, anyway. So, yeah, I asked Butch if he would help, so he and your dad went out there a few weeks ago to check it out, and made a great deal for it. It was a little out of my price range, so your parents and all your brothers chipped in with me, and we got it. You go to pick it up on Monday. The guy said he can't wait to meet you."

I can't believe she did this...for me? This has to be the best gift anyone has ever gotten me. She knows me better than anyone ever will.

"Angel." I grin, reaching for her, but she takes a quick step back.

I frown as she giggles. "Hold on, there's more," she says, dropping the poster on the ground to reveal herself clad in a sexy-as-fuck, cherry red, see-through lace lingerie—glowing with her twenty-two-week bump.

I growl, leaping to my feet and snatching her by the waist. I hoist her into my arms by her ass and wrap her legs around me. "You're perfect, baby, you know that?"

I love you.

Twenty-One.

Maci

"Butch is pushing hard for a rugged, manly name for the baby." Cassidy sighs, sipping her peppermint mocha while leaning against the display at Cup O' Joe. "Ever since we found out it's a boy, he's been coming up with these insane names. I don't know where he comes up with this stuff."

I raise a brow. "Like what?"

I've been having a hard time myself picking a suitable name for my daughter—well, I've had one picked out since I was sixteen, but I'm not sure if it's still a good pick for my baby girl. And at twenty-six weeks today—a whopping six and a half months pregnant—I'd like to settle on a name before I buy any baby décor for the cabin.

I signed a year lease at the start of the new year, and with it being the end of March, I've still got another nine months in my lease. Regardless of how many times Duke wants to say it's *not a big deal* to break the lease and move into the new house with him, it's a big deal to *me* when I'd be losing my security deposit and last month's rent.

He's been fighting me at every angle, but I don't feel comfortable with the idea of living in a house that's *his*. I mean, I love him—more than I've ever loved anyone. But I fear these last four months, I've been relying on him too much.

Centering myself, my day, my life—*everything*—around building a future with him. All I have is invested in *us*—something I swore I'd never let myself do again. Yet here I am, doing it again. And I'd be in a very vulnerable position if I were to move in before we know what kind of relationship we'll have once the baby arrives.

What happens if it all goes south? My daughter and I will be homeless, scrambling to find a place to go. I can't let that happen—not now, not ever.

Duke...loves me, I think. He hasn't said it, even though I've told him every day since Valentine's Day. He tells me he feels the same way about me, that he's just *having a hard time finding the words*.

Well, he didn't have a hard time finding the right words to convince me to give us a chance. Or making me fall madly in love with him. *What if he's just telling me what I want to hear?*

The thought alone makes my stomach ache.

"Buck, Gage, Bruce, Bruno... Blaze," Cassidy says.

Alison booms with laughter. "*Blaze*? No, he did not."

I smile. "I like Gage."

"That's the only one I told him I liked," Cassidy admits. "We did settle on the middle name, though. It's going to be Anthony, after my father."

"Gage Anthony Montgomery," Alison tests. "It has a nice ring to it."

"What was the boy name you had picked out, Maci?" Cassidy asks me.

"I didn't have one, but I always liked Mason."

"Have you picked any girl names yet?" Alison asks curiously. "Any ideas?"

I shrug.

"Oh, come on," Cassidy whines. "I know you've got ideas. I've always loved the name Renee. Butch even said he liked it if we ever have a girl."

"That's nice," I say, my phone dinging with a text on the side counter.

Duke: *What time do you get out of work?*

Me: *Half an hour.*

Duke: *I'm at the house. Rhett brought over some paint samples. You mind swinging by on your way home to take a look?*

I frown at the screen. He thinks he's being slick, but I know what he's doing.

Me: *I have to stop at the pharmacy to pick up more prenatal vitamins, then I can swing by if you want.*

Duke: *I'll see ya in a bit. Drive safe.*

"Oh, boy. I know that look." Cassidy laughs. "What'd Duke do now?"

I sigh. "Nothing, he just... He won't stop with this whole 'move into the new house with me' thing. And honestly...he's starting to get a little aggressive about it."

Alison's brow furrows. "Aggressive, really?"

"That's not like Duke," Cassidy says in concern.

"I know." My frown only deepens. "He doesn't understand why I think it's too soon."

"But you live together now?" Alison reasons. "Why can't you just move to the new house together? I thought everything was going well."

"It is. It's just... What if it flops after the baby comes?" I throw my hands in the air in dismay. "Babies bring a lot of new things to the table: stress, sleepless nights, financial aspects, schedule rearranging. Not to mention the strain it can put on a relationship."

"Have you talked to Duke about all this?" Cassidy asks.

"Of course, we have. All he says is, '*We're rock solid, baby, don't worry about it,*'" I say in my best Duke impression. Alison and Cassidy laugh. "But I *am* worried. Our relationship has been amazing so far. I don't want to break my lease, move in with him, have the baby, bring her home, then everything changes, and we break up. And where will I be? Rushing to find a place to go with a newborn at the last minute."

"Duke would *never* kick you and the baby out, Maci," Cass says sternly.

"I *know*. That's the problem. What if he ends up miserable, but won't dump me because he wouldn't want to put us out? I mean, I hate to say it, I really, really do, but..."

"It's not his baby," Alison says, and I cringe.

"Alison," Cassidy gasps.

I blow out a shaky breath. "No, she's right, it's not. My daughter isn't his responsibility, no matter how he sees it. It'd be irresponsible of me to expect Duke to keep us around out of the goodness of his heart for god knows how long until I was to find another place to live. I can't do that to him—to me. The cabin is a good space for now. It'll work until the end of my lease, then I'll find something bigger after that. Or, if we make it through the rough stuff in the beginning with the baby, maybe I'll move in with him... I don't know."

Cassidy puts her hands up as if to stop my mind from spiraling any deeper—too late. "This whole conversation is meaningless because you and Duke aren't breaking up. *Ever*. Duke loves you too much to let your relationship flop, Maci, seriously. This baby is his in his heart, and that's all that matters."

"He hasn't even said it back, Cass," I say, grabbing up my purse and sweater. I punch out for the day and walk around the counter. "I have to go. I'll see you guys later."

"Maci," she calls out to me, and I can hear the upset in her voice—but it's the truth.

I *have* to be smart about this. I can't put myself in the kind of place I was last year with Evan. Relying on him as my only form of support—emotionally, mentally, physically. The only thing I had control of was that I could support myself financially, and here, I can do that—by *not* moving into his house right away.

I need to do this on my own as best I can to preserve our relationship.

A while later I'm turning onto the long drive at Duke's property. The house looks great. Hunter green siding, brown roofing, stunning natural wood framed windows, and the gorgeous mahogany front door to match the covered wood beam wraparound porch.

It's grown into a rustic mountain lodge home with views to die for.

I bite my lip at the sight of a very large box perched in the back of Duke's truck.

It's the crib I ordered last week. "Shit."

The second I park the bay door to the garage opens, and the look on Duke's face says it all.

I get out and go to him. His towering frame imposing with his arms crossed over his chest and a heated scowl on his face. I peer around him at the open hood of the Chevelle and the engine sitting on a mount beside it.

"Did you finally get the rebuild kit in?" I ask, innocent as can be.

"The crib you ordered came today," he growls. *I guess we're getting right into it then.* "When were you going to tell me you started ordering stuff? And why was it delivered to the cabin and not here?"

"I found a crib I liked, and it was on sale, so I bought it," I say with a casual shrug.

His scowl doesn't waver at my 'it was on sale' reasoning. "Why didn't you tell me? I would've given you my card to charge it and had it shipped to the right damn place."

Now he wants to *pay* for the baby's stuff, too?

I scoff. "The *right place*? Really, Duke? We've talked about this. I'm—"

"No, Maci," he bites out. "You've rambled on and on with excuses for why you don't want to move into the house for two months. That's been the extent of the conversation."

"Excuses? Me thinking it's too soon to be moving into the house is *not* an excuse."

"Yeah, it fucking is," he snaps, gesturing to the cabin down the road. "We already live together. Why wouldn't we continue doing just that?"

"Because *Duke*—" I throw my hands in the air in frustration. "—I don't know if we can make it after the baby comes. Do you have any idea the percentage of relationships that end after the birth of a child? It's high, honey, *really* high."

His nostrils flare in anger. "You don't believe that would happen to us for a second, because it won't."

I shake my head. "You don't get it."

"Give me one good reason why we shouldn't move forward with everything we have to the new house," he demands. "We're together. We love each other. What's the problem?"

"Do you love me? Because I haven't heard you say it yet," I bite back, and regret hits me before I can stop myself. *Too far...*

His jaw clenches. "That's not fair, Maci, and you know it."

Tears sting my eyes, and I turn away. Why am I doing this to myself? I'm fighting him when all he wants is for us to be together.

"Angel." He sighs, reaching for me. I cover my face as I start to cry, and he holds me to his chest, rubbing my back soothingly. "You know how I feel about you."

I nod against him. "I-I know. I'm sorry."

"What's this really about?" he asks gently.

I bury my face into his chest.

Duke kisses the top of my head. "I get it. You don't want to have to rely on me when the baby comes if something were to happen between us." I peer up at him. "I get it, babe, I do. But that doesn't apply to us, all right? We're solid. More solid than anything I've ever had in my life. And if keeping the lease on the cabin as a backup plan is this important to you, then... Fuck it. We'll keep the cabin. The house isn't even close to ready to move in, the paint alone is going to take a week or more to air out before I want you in there."

I sniffle. "Do you mean that?"

"Yes," he says, brushing my hair out of my face. "But you've gotta promise me you'll give the house a chance. Stay here a few nights during the week and get a feel for the place. And we sleep together every night, no matter where it is. The cabin, here, wherever you want."

This man... "I love you."

He grins and leans down to kiss me. "And the crib is staying here."

I pout. "Duke."

"No, seriously, the crib *has* to stay here. I measured the bedroom at the cabin, and unless you want to put the baby in the living room by the fireplace, it ain't happening."

I scrunch my nose. "Are you sure? I thought if I pushed the bed up against the wall, I could fit the crib next to it."

He grumbles under his breath, and I fight down a smirk. "We'll see. Did you buy anything else?"

"A mattress for the crib, but that's it."

"All right, well, we should probably start a list, figure out everything we need, and keep me in the loop when you're buying things. But for now, if you don't mind, I'd like it if you could pick out a few paint colors for the house."

We're quick to agree on a majority of the paint samples—well, more like Duke asks me what I like, then just agrees with me. Same as he's done with everything else with his house.

And I do mean *everything*.

I point to a hideous brown for the upstairs master bathroom as a test. "I like this one."

Duke scoffs. "No, you don't."

"I do, too," I say stubbornly.

He narrows his eyes at me, keeping my gaze as he points to a beautiful rumba orange that I love. "You like this one." His tone stern, knowing—because he's right. I do.

"You can't just keep going with everything I pick, Duke," I huff. "Tell me which one you like. This is *your* house."

To my surprise, he looks irritated by my comment.

His jaw tightens. "This'll be *our* house. The sooner you accept that, the better. And I'd rather not have to repaint when you finally realize you don't like something I chose. Besides, I like everything you've already chosen, so it's a win-win."

I try to be annoyed, but I can't wipe this stupid smile off my face. "Fine." I point to the rumba orange. "This one."

He chuckles, pulling down the other paint samples and marking down 'master bath' on the orange. I follow him out through the master bedroom and across the hall to one of the spare rooms where there are easily over a hundred different paint samples taped up—all girly pinks and purples and a few neutral tones.

Tears threaten at the very sight.

Duke turns to me with a grin. "Like I said, I don't want to have to repaint."

Why does he have to make it so hard to be mad at him for longer than five minutes?

He's too good to be true.

He chuckles when I start to cry. "These pregnancy hormones are really gettin' to you today, aren't they?"

I stifle a laugh, dabbing my eyes. "You have no idea."

❧

"And that marks the end of today's class," the instructor of the birthing class announces. "Thank you everyone for coming, and I wish you all a smooth delivery ending in a healthy mommy and baby."

Sitting between Duke's legs on a yoga mat, I lean into him, sighing as he wraps his arms around me from behind. He rubs my seven-and-a-half-month bump. "Thirty weeks down, ten more to go," he whispers, kissing my temple.

Cassidy groans, rolling on her side. "Butch," she whines. "Help me."

He chuckles, helping her to her swollen feet. "Ready to go eat, Sunshine?"

She glares at her fiancé. "That's all I ever do is eat. Your damn son is turning me into a garbage disposal. I'm already bigger than Maci by a long shot."

"You're not *that* big, Cass," I say.

"The hell I'm not," she retorts. "I'm measuring four weeks ahead, Maci. *Four*. That's a whole month ahead of *you*. And you're like what, measuring a little behind?"

"Dr. Sanderson thinks she's going to be a tiny baby," I say, placing my hands over Duke's as little kicks and punches bump his hands. She loves it when he rubs my belly.

Cassidy scoffs, glaring at Butch. "I'm going to birth a linebacker because of you."

Butch grins smugly, wrapping his arms around her. "He's a healthy, happy boy growing inside of you, sweetheart. You can't be mad about that."

My stomach tightens painfully. I wince. The feeling is foreign, somewhere between an intense cramp and an ache. My entire body tenses as I suck in a sharp breath.

Duke's hands freeze on my belly, feeling how tense I've gotten. "Hey, you okay, doll?"

I nod, blowing out the breath long and slow. "Just a cramp," I say, glancing over my shoulder at him. "Can you help me up?"

He gets up and comes around to my front, helping me to my feet. He watches me closely as I hold a hand under my belly with a scrunch of my face at the uncomfortable, cramping pain.

"What is it?" he asks. "What's wrong?"

I shake my head, not having the words to explain it.

"Ah, I see we're having some Braxton Hicks over here," the instructor sing-songs. "How far along are you, hon?"

"Thirty weeks," I reply, blowing out a tense breath.

"You're having false labor. Right now?" Cassidy squeals, rushing over to me in a quick waddle.

"False?" Butch questions in alarm. "What is false about it?"

"Before *true* labor begins, women can experience what we call false labor or Braxton Hicks," the instructor states. "These contractions vary based on the mother. Some experience light cramping, others can be more intense, simulating labor contractions. All good signs that your body is prepping."

"Does it hurt?" Cassidy asks, poking my stomach. "You're so tense."

I swat her hand away. "It doesn't feel good if that's what you're asking."

"Remember the breathing we worked on today. Controlled breaths can be very helpful, regardless of the level of discomfort," the instructor tells me before excusing herself to where the next class is arriving.

Duke takes my free hand, looking me over in concern.

"I'm okay," I say, the tension in my body finally releasing. *Thank god.* That was getting a little much.

His brow furrows, not believing me. "Are you sure? We can head home if you want. Baby shopping can wait."

"Are you kidding, honey?" I snort. "If anything, she just told us we better get our butts in gear."

"How bad was it? Scale of one to ten," Cassidy asks eagerly.

I stare down at my belly. "Maybe a five? It was like a bad period cramp, but more tense and uncomfortable."

"We can buy everything online," Duke says in a panic. "We should get you home to lay down and rest."

"I'm fine, Duke. It's gone now. And I want to pick out her coming home outfit. Oh, and get one of those mink soft blankets for her."

"Food first," Cassidy states firmly, earning a booming laugh from Butch. She smiles at him as he takes her hand and walks to the exit.

I go to follow them when Duke holds me back. I look up at him, his dark eyes a mixture of emotions—worry being the most prominent. "Maci…"

I get on my tippy toes and give him a quick kiss. "We're okay," I whisper. "She's staying put for now. I promise."

Silence lingers between us for a moment before he huffs, "Two stores max after lunch. I don't want you walking around all day if you're going to be hurting with these false labor pains."

I beam. "Yes, sir."

He sighs, shaking his head with a play of a smile. "I mean it, angel. I don't want you overdoing it."

I tug his arm, to bring him in for another kiss. "I won't. And if I do, I'll have you to carry me to the car," I tease.

He chuckles. "Always."

Twenty-Two.

Duke

I TRAIL MY TONGUE up and down her dampening slit, eliciting a soft moan from Maci.

"Duke."

I growl into her pussy and lick her slow and sweet. Her legs tremble, and she grips the bedsheets. I slip a finger into her tight, dripping cunt. I suck her swollen clit between my lips and pump my finger. Her body arches.

"Oh, Duke, yes-yes-*yes*." She writhes in pleasure as her walls begin to tighten.

My cock throbs to be inside her as she comes on my face and hand, her hot pussy bursting with her release. I grin into her, licking up every last bit.

I crawl up the bed beside her as she rolls onto her side. She holds her leg up so I can rub the head of my cock over her soaking entrance, trailing her juices up to her tight little asshole.

"Don't even think about it," she warns with a breathy laugh.

Amusement rumbles in my chest as I kiss her neck. "I can't help it. Every bit of you is fuckin' sexy," I growl, pushing into her from behind. We moan in unison as I fully seat myself inside of her. "Goddamn, angel."

I reach around to her core and rub at the soft sides of her clit. She pushes her sweet ass against me, sending my cock deeper. My hips move to a slow, steady rhythm.

"Right there," she gasps, and I can feel she's close once again.

I groan, burying my face into her neck—kissing and nipping and breathing her in. My orgasm begins to creep up on me, and I buck my hips forward, slapping her ass with the force of it.

Her whimpers and moans urge me to a punishing pace as I fuck her. I slide an arm under her head and wrap my hand around her neck, forcing her to look at me. I pin her with a pinch of her clit, a hand on her throat, and my cock pulsing deep inside her.

The slick, snug walls of her cunt flutter around my length and pull my release to the brink. I come hard, groaning her name.

My movements slow as the raw tension of our combined orgasms washes over me in a calming wave. I pant, kissing her before I drop my hands and allow her to get up—giving her ass a light tap as she does.

She peers back at me. "You better stop, or we'll never make it to Cassidy's baby shower," she says, sashaying to the bathroom.

I grin at the sight of my cum sliding down her luscious thighs.

"You know, that's probably the last time you'll be able to come in me," she calls out.

I get up to follow her. "Why?"

She turns on the shower. "Dr. Sanderson said once my cervix starts to open we have to be careful, otherwise I can get an infection. Sex is fine, but no jizz."

"Jizz," I snort, and she giggles. "All right. Anything else we need to start being careful of?"

"I'm not sure," she says, throwing her beautiful, auburn hair up on top of her head. "We can ask her tomorrow at my appointment."

I wait for her to step into the shower before doing the same. She balks when I do. "Babe, this shower isn't big enough for the two of us anymore with my belly."

I scoff. "Sure it is." Her eight-month bump presses against my abdomen with my back nearly touching the far wall. Water pours between us and down my neck and shoulders. It's a tight squeeze, but manageable. "See?"

She bursts out laughing. "You're crazy."

"Crazy for you." I chuckle, and she pecks my lips.

Our relationship has been a dream these last six months. Except for the bickering over moving into the new house, which I've decided to let go...for now. The house has been done, furnished, and ready to live in for the last four weeks. And per our compromise, we've been staying there a few nights a week, building a comfortable feel for the place.

I know she's nervous about letting the cabin go because of the safety net it provides, but she needs to decide where we'll be bringing the baby—sooner than later. We've bought everything she and the baby will need and, whether she realizes it or not, the majority is at the new house. Including her storage pod from Oklahoma.

If she's leaning toward the house, she hasn't confirmed it. I'm doing my damnedest not to pressure her and ruin the momentum we have going. But fuck... It's hard when she's been doing that 'nesting' my mother warned me about, getting things ready for the baby's arrival at both places.

It's taking a lot out of her. I've already convinced her to cut her hours at the coffee house to stay off her feet, and the resort narrowed down the yoga classes to only three per week. Everything is falling into place.

Because with the help of Cassidy—and even my brother—I've bought an engagement ring for Maci. One I hope she'll love enough to wear for the rest of her life as my wife.

Fuck. *My wife.* I never thought I'd say those words again.

I've talked it out with Butch, my father, my mother—Maci deserves it all. Her *and* the baby. And I know in my gut, as much as I loved Rachel, and I always will, I feel it in my heart... Maci is my true soulmate.

The light of my life has been these last six months with her, and I wouldn't change a thing—not her, not the baby, not the biological father. Because all of that brought her here to me.

So, with my plan in place to take Maci away on a surprise getaway next week, I'll be getting down on one knee to propose for the last time to the woman I love.

So why can't I tell her I love her?

My mother says it's fear that I'll lose her the way I lost Rachel if I do. She's probably right, but no matter how I feel about it, hearing those words will mean everything to Maci. And proposing to her before the baby comes will show her *exactly* how serious I am about being there for her—no matter what.

Helping my *stunning*, soon-to-be fiancée out of the passenger side of her car—since she hates me having to lift her to get in my truck now—I take in how gorgeous she truly is. The light grey, body-hugging dress molds around her curves and swollen stomach to stop just past her knees. Her hair cascades in waves down to the middle of her back, her full lips curling into the same smile that captured my heart on the side of the road just outside of town.

"What?" she asks, catching me staring at her.

I grin. "You look beautiful."

Her face lights up. "Thank you. You don't look too bad yourself, hot stuff." She makes a show of biting her lip and ogling my jeans, boots, and a black T-shirt.

"I'm a slimeball compared to you, angel." I chuckle, retrieving the gift bag from the backseat.

She tugs on a thin black sweater, taking my hand as we walk up to my parents' house where over thirty cars line the driveway. A large tent sits in the front yard with several shades of blue balloons and '*baby boy*' decorations all over the place.

My mother offered to throw Maci a baby shower, but she declined. We'd already bought the big ticket items, and between the women at the coffee shop and my mother buying baby clothes and accessories along with everything they've been doing for Cassidy—we're set to dress this little girl for a solid year in different outfits every damn day.

She isn't even born, and she's already got a *bow drawer*.

Butch is the first to greet us. "Thank fuck you're here."

I raise a brow. "Everything all right?"

My brother huffs, glancing over his shoulder. "If I have to hear one more *fun fact* about labor and how you can shit during it, I'm going to lose *my* shit."

Maci smothers a laugh.

"Yeah, well, it could happen." I hold up the giant gift bag in hand. "Where do you want this?"

Butch leads us to a table under the open white tent, and before I know it, Cassidy is pulling Maci away for pictures. I grin at her beautiful smile and the sound of her priceless laugh—the one where she can't help but snort a little.

She's perfect.

"Did you pick up the ring yet?" Butch asks quietly as we stand side by side.

"Not yet," I say. "I'll get it at the end of the week before we leave. I don't want her to find it beforehand."

"Cassidy's already talking about a double wedding." Butch shakes his head. "And since she can't tell anyone else about it for another week...she's been talking my ear off." His mouth lifts at the corner, a sure sign he doesn't mind it one bit.

"Sounds like Cass."

"You busy tomorrow?" he asks. "The crib came. Could use a hand putting it together."

Maci and Cassidy start making their way back to us.

"Maci's got an appointment tomorrow, but we can stop by after."

"Hey, Duke." Cass smiles, grabbing Butch's hand. "We're going to do pictures before we eat. You, too, Duke. I want you and Maci with us," she demands, dragging her fiancé along behind her.

Maci takes my hand. "We better follow before she comes back for us."

I playfully smack her ass and earn myself a sexy laugh from her. "After you, gorgeous."

We go through the motions of taking pictures, then eat. There's a lot of mingling between my family, Cassidy's family, and friends. The conversations between nearly fifty women in one place seem to go on forever. There's a bunch of games and the number of gifts...

I didn't realize how big a baby shower really is.

"So, have you settled on a name yet, Cass?" Lily asks. "And please, don't say Blaze."

Butch scowls.

Cassidy beams. "We did. Gage Anthony Montgomery."

My mother claps. "Oh, I love it."

"Blaze is cool, though," I chime in, and Maci swats me on the arm.

Butch cocks a grin. "I tried to tell her. He'd be an even bigger badass than he already is with a name like Blaze."

Cassidy rolls her eyes. "Don't encourage him, Duke."

"What about you, Maci?" Lily asks.

I squeeze her thigh as she sits next to me with her arm wrapped around my forearm, deepening her hold on me. "I've got a few I like," she admits, "but only one's been sticking out to me."

My ears perk up. She hasn't told me she settled on one. She's bounced a few ideas off me, but I told her it's whatever she wants. She'll pick something perfect all on her own.

Cassidy sits up straighter. "*Please*, tell me. I've been begging you for months."

"Okay, okay," Maci starts, and everyone gives her their undivided attention. "Olivia Grace."

My chest tightens.

Olivia Grace. You'll be as beautiful as your mother.

Cassidy gasps, on the verge of tears. "It's perfect."

My mother fans her eyes. "Oh, boy. I'm losing it here, kids."

Butch tilts his head. "That's a good one. I mean, not as badass as Blaze..." he trails off with a chuckle when Cassidy begins full-blown crying over Maci's announcement.

My angel sniffles beside me, and I turn my attention to her. "Aw, doll, don't cry," I say, hugging her tight to my side.

She blows out a shaky breath, dabbing under her eyes with a napkin. "Sorry. I've just never said it out loud like that before," she whispers. "It's so official, you know? She'll be here in a few short weeks."

I kiss her temple, my heart pounding at the thought. "She will be."

With the party coming to an end, people disperse to say their long goodbyes and well wishes. Maci covers her mouth on a yawn as I rub her slightly swollen ankles. "You about ready, darlin'?" I ask. She nods, pulling her legs off my lap.

Standing with her, she says, "I'm just going to run in and use the bathroom quick."

"Come on, I'll take you," I say, holding her hand and leading us inside. She opts to use the downstairs bathroom to avoid the stairs. "I'll wait in the kitchen for you. Maybe steal a few peanut butter cookies for the ride home." I wink.

She smiles. "See if there's any pie left. Cassidy said she bought two—one for me."

"You got it."

I head into the kitchen, where Lily and Grandma Judy are standing beside the island. My father's perched on a stool—flat-out hiding. I grip his shoulder as I pass by. "Hiding out, Pop?" I chuckle, grabbing a Ziploc bag to properly steal these cookies.

My father laughs huskily. "Damn right, I am. I figured you and Butch would've been in here with me hours ago."

Lily shakes her head. "You'll be paying for not going out there to join the party later. Mom's already made a few comments under her breath."

My father waves her off. "She'll live."

"And how are you and Maci doing, dear?" Grandma Judy asks me.

"We're doing great," I say, loading up a dozen cookies in the baggie and tossing them on top of the untouched peanut butter pie that has a sticky note on top with Maci's name on it.

"Did you kids move everything into the house yet?" my father asks. "Your mother said y'all were transitioning."

Almost. "We're working on it."

"Good for you, Duke." Grandma Judy nods sternly. "I wasn't sure about this Maci-girl in the beginning, but your mother assures me she's a good replacement for Rachel."

"Grandma." Lily gapes in shock—not that it's a surprising statement coming from her. Gran has always been nasty when it comes down to her morals.

"No one's replacing anyone," I bite out.

My grandmother stands a little straighter, her features stoning at my hard tone. "I only hope the poor girl knows she has big shoes to fill. Rachel was a lovely woman. But I suppose replacing her and the baby you lost with Maci and her bastard child is God's way of picking up the pieces."

Motherfu—

"Christ, Judy." Pop shakes his head.

My jaw tightens. *You can't tear your grandmother's fucking head off*, I tell myself repeatedly...even if the urge is still there. *Who the hell told her anyhow?* I snatch the pie and cookies and turn to leave when my heart drops to the pit of my stomach.

Maci's standing in the hall, fresh tears glimmering in her emerald eyes, and her expression is...devastated.

My mind races back to everything she could've heard from my bitch of a grandmother, and my world stops when she puts a protective hand over her belly and a hand over her mouth before darting back into the bathroom.

No. No. No—Fuck!

Twenty-Three.

Maci

"Babe, open the door." Duke bangs on the bathroom door for the tenth time, and my heart breaks into a million pieces.

I'm a replacement...again. My baby girl is a replacement.

It all makes sense now. Why Butch was so concerned in the beginning. I thought he was just being overprotective of his brother, that he was worried since this is the first relationship he's been in since his wife died, but it wasn't that at all.

Rachel was pregnant.

Is that why Duke was all over me? Worrying about me, taking care of me? He said I was his...me and my baby.

He rebuilt everything he had—everything he lost.

We're replacements.

I pull myself off the ground to stand on unsteady feet. A choked sob escapes me at the jostle of the door handle and Duke's begging from the other side.

My stomach knots. My heart hits the floor. Every word he's ever said to me is a kick to my chest. How could I be so blind?

Gathering myself, I wash my hands and fix my makeup. With tears still streaming down my flushed cheeks, I unlock the door to the face that's brought me nothing but comfort for months. So many emotions swirl in his dark eyes...I don't know what to do with them.

"Maci, I—"

I put a hand up to stop him. "Not here," I say quietly.

His jaw tightens, but he nods. I wait in the hall while he retrieves something from the kitchen, but when Lily's worried gaze locks with mine, I have to turn away from breaking down any further.

He comes back to my side with a pie and bag of cookies, and when he reaches for my hand...I let him take it. Because as bad as I want to push him away, this is Cassidy's baby shower. And the last thing she needs is me making a scene when the day's gone so beautifully for her.

We walk to the table to grab my sweater and purse. Hoping to leave without having to say anything to anyone, I fight to control my emotions when the hope is short-lived.

Butch lifts his chin. "You guys heading out?"

"Yeah," Duke grunts.

"Oh, Maci, are you okay?" Cassidy asks gently, noticing my puffy eyes, I'm sure.

I wave her off, forcing a smile. "I'm fine. Just got a little sick is all."

His brother's brow furrows as he shares a look with Duke.

"Well, I hope it wasn't anything you ate," Cassidy says with concern.

I keep a pained smile as I tug on my sweater. "No. I think it's just a little late afternoon sickness. They say it can come back toward the end." I clear my throat and glance at Duke. "Ready?"

His jaw ticks with whatever he's dying to say to make this all go away, but there's nothing he can say to make this one better.

We say our goodbyes, and Duke helps me into the car. We drive the three minutes to the cabin in silence. When he parks my car beside his truck, he kills the engine with a sigh. "Maci."

My bottom lip quivers as I scramble to gather my things and get out. "Please, don't." He jumps out after me as I make my hurried way to the cabin, wanting nothing more than to put some space between us.

"I don't know what you heard, angel, but you have to know everything out of my grandmother's mouth is said with malicious intent."

I put my hand out. "Give me my k-keys, Duke."

He doesn't acknowledge my request and simply opens the front door. When he holds it open, I enter—only to stop in the door frame and block him from following me.

"Maci—"

"I think you should stay at the house tonight," I say with as much strength as I can muster.

His brow furrows as he reaches for me, but I take a step back, gripping the door as if it's the only thing keeping me upright. "I'm not going anywhere, angel," he growls. "You're upset. I'm not leaving you."

"Is it true?" I ask weakly. I need to know. It might not seem like a big deal, but I swore to myself I'd never let anyone make me feel this way again—inferior, not good enough, second best... Not after Evan. "Was she pregnant when she died?"

He grits his teeth. "Maci, that's not—"

"Is it true?" I cry, clutching my belly to protect my daughter from this heartbreak.

His dark eyes pain as he snatches me by my waist before I have time to protest. I try to push him off, my entire body wracking with sobs. "Let me go..."

"Listen to me, please," he says, holding me close. "Yes, she was only six weeks at the time—we never even made it to the first appointment. It was five years ago, Maci, you have to know it has nothing to do with us now. You could *never* be a replacement, beautiful. Olivia isn't a replacement."

I shake my head, crying at his use of my unborn daughter's name.

"I love you, Maci," he says for the first time. "I love both of you."

I fall into him, burying my face in his chest. He holds me uncomfortably tight, his face in the crook of my neck, leaving a trail of light kisses. "I love you so much..."

For *months* I've wanted to hear those words—the same way I feel for him—*from* him. And now...they feel tainted. My heart aches.

I gently push him away, and he pulls back, his eyes glossy with unshed tears—the sight only makes this harder. "You should go," I force myself to say.

"No," he snaps. "Angel, don't."

"I-I need some time," I say, and it's true. I need to process this—all of it. "Please."

He reaches for me, but I step back. "Maci, don't do this, please. Whatever you want to know, I'll tell you—everything, I swear. I love you."

My entire world shatters, and I feel like I'm spinning out of control. *Breathe, Maci.* I suck in a deep breath, and take three steps back, leaving Duke with empty arms as I close the door and lock it.

I love you, too.

"As many hours as you can give me for the next few weeks would be great, Peggy," I say, cashing out a customer at Cup O' Joe. Once the customer leaves, I glance over my shoulder, and her expression tells me I'm *not* getting those hours.

"You're nearly thirty-eight weeks pregnant, dear. I don't think being on your feet all day is a good idea," Peggy scolds.

Under normal circumstances, I'd agree with her. But it's been four days, six hours, and seventeen minutes since I told Duke I needed a break—time to clear my headspace, to figure out what I want to do. To see if I can move past this sinking feeling in my heart.

It's not him, it's...*me*.

He didn't leave that night. Opting to bring my dessert inside with a note telling me he's here if I need anything, he slept in his truck right outside my front door—the same way he has for the last four nights.

He's been calling and texting every day, wanting to know how I'm feeling, if I'm okay, and how my appointment went. He shows up at the coffee shop when I'm working and lingers, but doesn't push to talk. He's always...*there*. For me, I suppose.

Every night, the low rumble of his truck is outside the cabin, and I feel like a monster.

If it was anyone else, I would've called the police for stalking, but it's Duke—caring, sweet, a little crazy, overprotective, obsessive *him*.

Who doesn't seem to understand the definition of giving someone space.

"I could use the money," I say quietly.

The bell over the front door chimes, and Cassidy storms in with Butch trailing behind her. "Maci," she barks, and I tip my head to the side in confusion at her aggressive tone.

"You're not on the schedule today, are you, Cassidy?" Peggy asks, also confused.

"No, I'm not, Peg," she says, her heated glare locked on *me*. "I have a bone to pick with a certain pregnant *chick*."

"Sunshine." Butch sighs heavily. "You can't—"

"Shut it," she snaps at him, and Butch regards me with an expression I can only read as telling me to 'brace for impact.'

Oh, boy.

"What the hell is your problem, huh?" she shouts at me, and I cringe. "You don't reply to his texts, you don't answer his calls. Duke is absolutely *broken*. And don't even try to tell me for a second you're not either. I know you've been hiding in the backroom on your breaks crying. Why are you dragging this out? You're only hurting yourself and your daughter."

"Cassidy, it's not that simple," I try to say, but it's clear—she's not having any of it.

"Duke is your support. He's been there for every appointment, every birthing class. And now you're going to go and have this baby *without* him?"

Her words are like a punch to the gut, and my stomach twists painfully.

Butch extends an arm in front of her chest as she takes a step toward the counter.

"You think I want to do this without him, Cass?" I say. "I don't want to do this with anyone but him. I love him with all my heart. But he lied to me. He should've told me Rachel was pregnant when she died. Do you have any idea how our relationship looks now? Me, the baby, living together since day one. All of it."

Cassidy shakes her head. "I do know. And you have every right to be upset with him, but you have to understand." Her voice lowers. "No one knew she was pregnant until after she was gone. Duke only ever told Butch and his parents."

"All right. I think that's enough pregnant smackdown for one day," Butch grumbles, gently ushering her back while eyeing the few shocked customers watching on.

It's a miracle someone doesn't have their phone out recording.

Cassidy swats his hand away. "I'm not done," she declares. "What are you so afraid of? Duke was ready to give you the world, Maci. The whole *world*. And you do *this* to him?"

I start to cry, because...she's right. And I know it, too.

"Grandma Judy is a horrid old hag. She can't stand to see anyone happy, so she preys on sensitive topics and situations to get her rocks off," she announces. "Judy only found out because she eavesdropped on a private conversation between Duke and his mother. He was going to tell you. You know he would never lie to you; he loves you *so* much, Maci. The man is devastated."

"I love him, too," I sniffle, taking the napkin Butch hands me.

Cassidy waddles around the counter, engulfing me in a hug. I hug her back as best we can with our large bellies pressed against each other. "He needs you, Maci. Probably more than you'll ever know. And you *have* to know you're not some twisted replacement family he chose five years later."

I pain a laugh. "I know, it's just—"

"No," she says, stopping me when she swipes the tears from my cheeks. "You and Duke belong together. You know it, I know it, Butch knows it." Her fiancé grunts from behind her. "Everyone in this Podunk town knows it. And as horrible as this might sound... I think if Rachel were here, she would know it, too."

I nod vigorously, blowing out a shaky breath as I peer out the front bay windows of the coffee shop, but Duke's truck isn't there. "Where is he?" I ask, looking to Butch.

He pulls out his phone. "Wherever the hell he is, I'm sure we can get him here."

"I told you she just needed a swift kick in the ass, honey." Cassidy smiles at Butch who just shakes his head and smirks.

An intense pain grips me.

I hiss, clutching my belly with one hand and holding the counter with the other. My back tenses as a dampness forms between my legs.

Oh, my— Did I just...pee myself?

Cassidy rests a gentle hand on my back. "Maci? What's— Oh my god, your water broke!"

I wince as another *real* contraction hits me. "No." I stare at the wet crotch of my leggings. "She can't. It's too soon. I'm not ready," I say, but a wave of pain hits me, and my knees buckle.

"Butch," Cassidy yelps, and he's racing around the counter.

"Everyone out," Peggy shouts. "We're closed. Out, out—Go." She rushes to usher people out the door with their coffees in hand.

I clutch my belly while Butch holds me upright. "Breathe, Maci," he tells me. Cassidy takes his phone and keys, scurrying ahead of us to hold the door.

"I need Duke," I cry.

"I'm trying," Cassidy says, her phone pressed to her ear. "Shit. He's not answering..."

I can't do this without him.

Twenty-Four.

Duke

"Fuck," I roar, whipping the wrench across the garage. It hits the wall with an echoing clang. I stalk out the open garage door, and I head to the house—*my* house that was supposed to be *ours*. Maci and me.

Why didn't I tell her?

She had every right to know. And I kept it from her.

I fucked up. And it might have cost me the woman I want to spend the rest of my life with. Because she's it for me. I'd rather die alone than be with anyone else.

I kick off my boots at the door. Everything is a memory that reminds me of her. From picking out the cabinets, the countertops, to the paint, and flooring. Laughing until we cried over shit-stain brown carpet.

My chest clenches.

We should be on our babymoon getaway getting ready for dinner at a fancy, high-rise restaurant. The place where I was going to propose. Not...*this*. Where we're taking—what? A break? Space? I don't even know anymore.

I already feel like a stalker. I've been sleeping in my truck outside the cabin every night. Checking in on her at work, at home—I've followed her to the damn gas station, for fuck's sake.

I'm losing it.

I go upstairs to my room to grab my phone off the charger when the same sight that's been tearing me up inside catches my eye. Not able to stop myself, I walk across the hall into the pastel purple room—the matching wooden crib, dresser, changing table, the fuzzy purple rug, the decorative flowers and butterflies on the wall, the baskets of baby clothes that still need to be put away...and the glider rocking chair I put together last night.

My entire body hurts being in this room without Maci by my side.

I love her so much it hurts.

My gaze lands on the curtain and rod that needs to be hung. I wonder if I should do it while I'm in here, or if it even matters anymore.

A glance out the window shows a cloud of dust forming as my brother's truck peels in the driveway. My brow furrows when he throws the truck in park, jumps out, and races over to the garage.

I scowl. What the hell does he want now?

I tug on my boots and step outside. "Where the fuck have you been?" he barks out, jogging toward me. "I've been calling you for the last hour."

"Phone is on the charger," I grunt.

"Maci's at the hospital. She's in labor."

Time stops.

"Yeah, exactly," he grumbles. "Get in the truck. We need to go. Now."

A moment later, we're on the road driving to the hospital. Butch's phone rings, and he answers. "Yeah, I got him. We're on our way," he says. "We'll be there as fast as we can." He hangs up and hits the gas.

"Is she okay? What happened? What'd she say?" I rapid fire. Her due date isn't for another two weeks. Dr. Sanderson told us she might go late due to Olivia being on the smaller side... *Maci must be terrified*. My heart pounds at the thought.

"My future wife is what happened," my brother says with a rough chuckle. "I told her to stay out of it, but she was driving me off the wall worrying about you and Maci. So, I drove her to the coffee shop. Long story short, Maci's water broke, and they're saying she's moving fast."

"Fast? What does that mean?"

Butch shakes his head. "I don't know, man. That's what they said when we got her to the hospital. She was...in a lot of pain. Cassidy was freaking out trying to reach you. I...didn't know what else to do."

My leg jumps in time with my racing heart. "You got her to the hospital safe, bro. That's all you could do."

Butch whips around the loop at the front entrance, and I jump out before the truck comes to a full stop. I hit the elevator and get to the third-floor maternity ward. I look around, desperately trying to remember where they said to go during the tour we took four months ago.

A nurse buzzes me in, and I dart to the front desk. "Maci Baker. She was brought in an hour ago. She's thirty-seven weeks, four days. Where is she?"

The nurse nods, typing on the computer, and popping her chewing gum louder than anyone legally should be allowed to.

I don't have time for this.

A cry down the hall catches my attention, and I run toward it on instinct alone.

"Sir. Sir, you can't go back there," the nurse shouts, but I don't stop.

Barreling into room eight, I lay sight to Maci doubled over on the edge of the hospital bed, clutching her belly in a pale pink gown. She's hooked up to several machines as Cassidy holds a bucket in front of her.

"Maci," I pant, rushing to her side.

"Excuse me, sir, you can't—" a nurse in the room starts.

"He's the father," Cassidy states, glaring at the nurse.

Maci peers up at me. "Duke," she cries, reaching for me.

My chest floods with emotions when I wrap my arms around her—a piece of my heart sliding back into place. "I'm right here, angel," I say. "Everything's going to be okay."

"Here comes another one," the nurse announces, watching a monitor off to the side.

Maci squeezes me tight with a hiss of pain. "It hurts."

I rub her back, feeling how tense she is. "I know, doll. Breathe through it. Remember those classes? All that breathing they told you to do." She nods against me and takes a deep inhale. "In through your nose, out through your mouth."

She does her breathing, her arms squeezing my neck, and her forehead pressed against my chest. I rock her from side to side—I saw it in a movie once, and it seems to be doing something because she relaxes into me.

"You're doing great, Maci," the nurse tells her. "It's coming down now."

Maci blows out a long breath before leaning back to look at me. Her plump bottom lip quivers as her gaze darts over my face. I missed those big, green doe eyes. "I'm so sorry."

"Shhh." I push the hair out of her face that's fallen from her messy bun. "You have nothing to be sorry for, beautiful. This is all my fault. I'm sorry I didn't tell you sooner," I say. "But believe me when I say this—you mean *everything* to me, Maci. You could never replace anyone. You're the best thing that's ever happened to me, angel. I love you. And I want to spend the rest of my life proving it to you."

She takes my scruffy, unkept face in her hands, and kisses me softly in response.

I don't think I'll ever get tired of her touch, her scent, her kiss—her love. *Her.*

"I love you, too," she whispers against my lips, and I feel it...

This is what forever feels like.

"We've got another one coming," the nurse says, and Maci tenses as she works through her breathing.

"How far apart are we, Debbie?" Dr. Sanderson asks as she hurries into the room.

"Contractions are two minutes apart and just shy of a minute long."

"All right, Maci. I'm going to have you finish this contraction, then I need you to lie back and we'll check you again," Dr. Sanderson says.

I help Maci to lie down, holding her hand as Dr. Sanderson checks her. "Eight centimeters dilated. Head is down." She pushes on her stomach and shakes her head.

"Can I get the epidural now?" Maci pleads, squeezing my hand.

Dr. Sanderson pains a smile. "Oh, we're long past that, dear."

Maci whimpers when the nurse announces another contraction. Another nurse arrives to prep the room for delivery. Maci shifts onto her left side, a death grip on both my hands while doing her breathing as best she can. Cassidy's holding a cool cloth to her forehead, and I'm doing my damnedest to stay strong for her—but I'm freaking out on the inside.

"When did you start having contractions, Maci?" Dr. Sanderson asks, staring at a paper in hand.

Maci hisses. "I-I don't know. The last few days, I guess? I had a few light ones this morning. I thought they were Braxton Hicks, though."

Dr. Sanderson walks around to face Maci. "I need you to listen to me as best you can, okay?" she starts, her tone serious in a calming way that only puts me on high alert. "What's happening now is what we refer to as precipitous or rapid labor. That's why you're having such intense contractions. Your body is ready to force this baby out one way or another. Are you feeling the urge to push?"

Maci nods vigorously, her nails digging into my forearm as she blows out a jagged breath.

"You need to work through the contractions. Don't push until you're fully dilated. If you try now, you'll risk tearing or harming the baby. Do you understand?"

"Y-Yes."

"Now, you're a little early, and that's okay. The baby will be fine, but I need you to understand she's going to be small, Maci."

Maci nods, and Dr. Sanderson shifts her attention to the nurses, instructing them to get NICU on-call and ready for the baby if needed.

"Duke," Maci says in a hushed whisper. "I'm scared."

I kneel beside her. "I know, angel." Her body starts to tremble as another contraction hits her. I rub her back, rocking her as she holds onto me. "You can do this, beautiful," I say, kissing her temple. "I'll be right here with you."

"But we didn't install the car seat yet," she softly cries.

I fight back a chuckle. "I'll take care of it."

"I missed you."

"Angel, I miss you every second of every minute when I'm not with you," I tell her. "Enough to become a damn stalker according to Butch."

"Maybe just a little bit." She laughs lightly. "But I liked it."

I chuckle. "Well, I hope you didn't like it too much. I've been miserable not being beside you."

Her glossy eyes shimmer. "I love you."

"I love you more," I say, kissing her tenderly.

Maci works through contractions for another painful half-hour before she's fully dilated and ready to push. But she's drained, exhausted from the intense, rapid labor. According to Dr. Sanderson, what Maci's doing now in a mere few hours, takes women nearly twelve hours or more to accomplish.

I asked if there was an Olympic race for giving birth this fast... Unfortunately, the dad joke was *not* well received.

With Cassidy holding one of Maci's legs, and me holding the other, Maci gets into position and starts to push.

"Perfect, Maci." Dr. Sanderson nods in encouragement while a nurse counts down on the contraction. "Just like that. Keep going, keep going."

She's panting, sweating, a cool cloth over her forehead as she works to push. After roughly a dozen or so pushes...

"We've got a full head of hair." Dr. Sanderson smiles. "Get ready, sweetie. Next contraction, I want a long, good push, okay?"

Maci has a look of pure determination on her beautiful face. And as the next contraction hits, she bears down, pushing long and hard with a silent scream in pain.

"Here she comes!" Dr. Sanderson catches Olivia. The faintest little wail fills the room, and my heart swells.

Maci sobs, reaching out as they place her baby on her bare chest. She's tiny and perfect in every way. A nurse wipes Olivia's eyes and face, draping warm blankets over them.

Maci glances at me with a beaming smile and tears in her eyes. I kiss her, tasting the salt of her tears mixed with mine. "I love you," I choke out, overcome with emotions.

She peers down at Olivia nestled between her breasts and tucks the blanket softly under her chin. "And we...love you," she whispers before gazing back at me.

I stand in front of the nursery room window, on strict orders from Maci to keep an eye on our little girl.

"She's tiny," Butch says lowly, his voice strained as we watch a nurse get a weight and length on Olivia. Her wails of protest are music to my ears.

Cassidy sniffles. "She's absolutely beautiful."

"Yeah. She is." I rub my face, fighting back the tears, but I can't.

Butch slaps a firm hand on my shoulder, bringing me in for a hug.

Cassidy fans her eyes. "Stop that." She laughs. "You guys are going to make me lose it all over again."

I sniff and wipe my eyes. "Think you can do me a favor, man?"

"You don't even need to ask, brother. Just tell me where it is."

Twenty-Five.

Maci

Nurse Debbie pushes a bassinet-like cart with my daughter—Olivia Grace—tucked soundly inside. She's wrapped up like an itty-bitty burrito in a white and pink striped blanket and a pale pink hat.

"We're ready to eat," Debbie announces, wheeling her to my bedside with Duke following closely behind.

He strides to my other side, and I smile, reaching for him. He leans down to kiss me, his eyes suspiciously puffy. "She did great. Hated every second of it." He grins.

The nurse hands me Olivia. "Hi, baby girl," I beam, cradling her tiny frame in my arms.

"Five pounds, seven ounces. Twenty inches long," Debbie tells me, helping me to position Olivia to latch onto my breast. She's a natural, of course, and Debbie excuses herself with a promise to return in a bit to check on us.

"She's so cute," I coo. I can't stop staring at her. She's the most adorable baby in the world, and not just because I made her.

Duke brings his chair close to the bed, his hand finding mine as we watch Olivia snuggle into my chest. "She's beautiful," he says. "Just like her mother."

We watch her for some time before Dr. Sanderson arrives with a clipboard in hand. "How are you feeling, Maci?"

"Sore," I reply honestly.

She goes over a slew of things we can do to help with my level of discomfort. When she sets the clipboard on the table beside me, she says, "This is the formal paperwork for the birth certificate. Take your time filling it out for accuracy. Check all spelling, first and last names. And make sure to get all the *parents'* information correctly before both *parents* sign."

A slow smile spreads across my face at her choice of words, and she spares a glance at Duke who hasn't taken his eyes off Olivia asleep on my chest.

She smiles, having to turn away when I catch the emotion welling in her eyes.

After she's gone, I point to the clipboard. "Can you grab that for me?" I ask.

"Sure, babe," he says, reaching over me, and as he goes to hand me the paperwork, I shake my head.

"I've listed you as my emergency contact since my first appointment here in Whitetail," I confess. "When I got here, they had me sign something in case anything was to happen to me during the delivery. Who would take Olivia if I didn't have the father of the child listed."

Duke's brow furrows.

I stare at her and start to cry. Duke takes my hand, and I smile. He fills my heart with so much love—the kind of love you want to keep for the rest of your life. And he'll be my daughter's first true love as well.

"I put your name down," I say. "If something were to happen to me, you would be the sole caretaker of Olivia."

He sucks in a breath. "Maci…"

"I know she's not yours," I choke out as tears fall from his strong dark eyes. "But she is. She's yours. You were made to be her dad."

His leg starts to jump as his chin quivers. He looks down at the paperwork in his hand. "I want to sign it," he says, glancing between me and Olivia. "But I need to do something first."

He sets the clipboard at my feet and stands. Pushing his chair back, he drops to one knee beside me.

"What are you—"

He pulls a little black box from his back pocket.

Duke takes my hand, clearing his throat. "From the second I saw you, stranded on the side of the road, I knew I was meant to find you," he says, and I choke on a laugh before a smile splits my face. "You went from being a stranger to my best friend, to the one I want to spend the rest of my days with. I love you with everything I have, Maci Ann Baker. And I'd love nothing more than to be your husband."

He opens the ring box to reveal a shimmering, oval-cut diamond sitting on a white gold band. "Angel, will you marry me?"

There isn't a doubt in my mind. I nod vigorously. "Yes."

My bossy, mountain of a mechanic leaps to his feet, his lips crashing against mine.

A slew of applause and cheers break us apart. I laugh at Butch, Cassidy, and Dr. Sanderson standing in the open doorway of the hospital room.

Duke takes my left hand and slides the ring on my finger. *A perfect fit.* I stare at him, wondering how I got so lucky to have found him. "I love you."

"I love *you*," he whispers, embracing our daughter and me.

When he pulls away, he grabs the clipboard. Having to swipe the back of his hand over his face as he tries to read the form through watery eyes. "Where am I supposed to sign on this thing?" he asks, peering at me with a widespread grin.

Dr. Sanderson tiptoes in to show Duke where to fill out his portion. And when he finally signs...everyone is in tears.

I shift Olivia in my arms. "Do you want to hold your daughter?"

He brings the chair to sit beside me as Dr. Sanderson takes Olivia from my arms and places her gently in Duke's. She looks so much tinier in his strong arms—the same arms that have protected me, cared for me, *loved* me all this time.

Cassidy shuffles over to me and hugs me tight. While Butch stands by his brother, gazing at Olivia in his arms. "Well, little lady." He cocks a half grin. "Guess I'd better get the shotguns ready for your daddy and all your uncles."

Cassidy rubs her belly. "Count on her cousin still cooking, too. She's too beautiful. You're seriously in trouble, Duke."

Duke grins from ear to ear. "Can't wait."

A knock at the door has us turning before it bursts open to a beaming Julie, Clayton, Rhett, Levi, Lily, and Parker holding a bouquet of flowers and a little pink teddy bear.

Pure joy envelopes me as my new family surrounds me with all the love and support I've ever wanted. Everything our daughter deserves.

Olivia Grace Montgomery.

All because my car broke down on the side of the road in Montana.

$Epilogue.$

Duke

Six months later...

"ARE YOU READY TO go, babe?" I holler, bouncing Olivia in my arms as we wait to load up and head to my parents for Christmas Eve.

Olivia turned six months old a few weeks ago, and she's thriving. She's still tiny for her age, but the girl is smart as a whip. With Maci's eyes, auburn hair, and beauty—she's the spitting image of her momma.

And I couldn't be prouder.

Maci and I tied the knot roughly three months ago. As soon as she was ready, we went to the courthouse. It wasn't the wedding

I expected her to want, but she told me repeatedly, all she wanted was to be married to me. So, we are. And Maci Baker is now Mrs. Duke Montgomery.

My wife.

Butch and Cassidy did the same thing after Gage was born—at the same time as us, I might add. Cassidy's convinced Maci to have a double formal wedding this upcoming summer. And I'm glad because Maci deserves the wedding of her dreams.

Not to mention, Butch is more than happy to split the bill with me.

Olivia yawns, snuggling into my neck, and my heart swells. She's wearing her plaid green Christmas dress with a matching bow and shoes I'm sure she'll kick off in the car on the short ride over.

"Coming," Maci calls, scurrying down the stairs. "I couldn't find her sweater for the life of me," she adds, Olivia's white button-up sweater in hand, and looking gorgeous as always.

Her hair cascades in waves, makeup done to the nines, wearing a tight, black sweater dress that hugs her curves in all the right ways. Black stockings—I plan to tear off later—and knee-high boots that make my cock twitch. "You look fuckin' amazing." I grin.

"Language," she snaps at me with a beautiful smile, her cheeks flushed. "I'm not having our sweet girl's first word be the f-bomb."

I chuckle deeply, shifting Olivia in my arms so her mother can put her sweater on. "I told you; it's going to be *Dada*. Bean and I already discussed it, she said she's gearing up for it soon."

Maci rolls her eyes. "I birthed her, it should be *Mama* first. Right, baby girl?" she coos, tickling Olivia and earning a heart-warming giggle from her.

"We'll see," I counter, buckling Olivia in her car seat.

"Did you talk to that new subletter for the cabin?" she asks, grabbing Olivia's diaper bag and favorite blanket. "She texted me a little bit ago and said she's willing to pay for the whole month of December if she can get in by tomorrow. She sounded kind of...desperate? I mean, she's willing to pay a whole month for only six days."

"Is this that Ryan-something you showed the cabin to?"

"Yes, Callie Ryan. She has the service dog."

"Beau said no pets," I grunt, lifting Olivia's car seat as Maci tucks her blanket around her.

"He's a service dog, honey." She frowns. "Beau could get sued if we deny her because of the dog. Besides, I met the dog. He's a giant teddy bear. Olivia was *obsessed* with him."

My ears perk up. "Does that mean Olivia can get a puppy?"

Maci narrows her eyes at me. "No."

I scoff. "You just said, she was *obsessed*. Why can't she have a puppy? She loves animals, especially dogs." Whenever she sees Cassidy's dog, Frankie, she loses her mind—squealing and giggling.

She's telling us she wants one, and my little girl gets whatever she wants.

"First off, stop saying it would be *her* puppy. She can't even say she wants a puppy," Maci says, tugging on her coat. "You're the one who wants a dog."

"And so does Olivia." I grin, carrying the car seat to my truck.

"We'll see," Maci repeats, mocking my tone from earlier.

I chuckle, strapping Olivia in and helping Maci in the front seat. We're off to my folks' place a moment later. "Does she at least have papers saying the dog *is* a service dog?" I ask. "Do we even know what kind of service dog he is?"

"She has papers. I think she called it a certification or licensing. She forwarded the paperwork with her rental application, but I don't remember what service he does. He wears this cute little vest and everything, though."

I nod. "All right, well, Rick moved out already so if she wants to get in there, she can. Ma cleaned out the place last weekend. We'll swing by on our way home and turn the heat up for her."

"I'll let her know now." Maci grabs her phone. "Have you talked to Beau about signing off on the lease so it can be between him and the renter instead of us?"

"Not yet. No one's been able to get ahold of him. I think Ma's hoping she'll hear from him today, but I doubt it."

"I can't believe he hasn't been home in almost three years. Don't they get leave or something?"

I turn into my parents' long drive, mindful of the bumps jostling the car seat in the back. "They do, but he doesn't use it. He'd rather see his brothers-in-arms get the chance to come home than go himself." Beau's always been the loner out of the five Montgomery brothers—something that I hope changes whenever he does decide to return home.

I park next to Butch's truck, and Maci slides out with the diaper bag in hand. I grab Olivia still in her car seat and the two bags of presents for Gage and Parker. The second we cross the threshold into the house, it's a commotion to see our girl for her first Christmas Eve.

There are pictures, dinner, pictures, dessert—*more* pictures.

I finally plop down on the couch beside Maci breastfeeding Olivia and throw my arm around her—living for every moment with my two favorite girls.

Butch walks in with his mini-him perched on his forearm. Gage is six weeks younger than Olivia, and easily twice the size of her. He's a real bruiser in his own right. It's no wonder Cassidy needed a C-section just to get the kid out.

"Did you want to feed him, babe?" Cassidy asks him, shaking a bottle with Frankie waddling behind her in his Christmas onesie from last year.

Butch tosses Gage in the air. "Yeah, I'll feed the little tank."

I snort. "*Little* tank is putting it mildly. Seriously, how much does he weigh now?"

"Twenty-two pounds," Butch announces proudly.

"He's already wearing twelve-month clothes," Cass adds. "I can only imagine how big he's going to get once he starts baby food in a few months. He eats like his damn father."

Butch grins wide, sitting next to Maci on the couch and popping the bottle in Gage's mouth. Cassidy perches on the arm of the couch beside him.

My mother comes into the living room, beaming as she snaps even *more* pictures. "We're going to do presents in a few minutes. Parker's just finishing up his gingerbread house," she tells us.

"Well, what's the verdict?" my father asks. "You kids having more grandbabies for us or what?" He chuckles.

"Hell yeah," Butch says, looking at his wife. "We're starting a football team."

Cassidy laughs. "Probably after the wedding. We'll wait a little bit, then start trying for another."

My mother nods eagerly before turning her attention to Maci and me. I look at my wife with a raised brow. We haven't talked about it, truthfully. She knows I'll give her anything she wants. And if that means Olivia is an only child, then so be it.

Maci smiles coyly, her eyes on me as she says, "Dr. Sanderson recommends waiting a full year. So, I'm thinking...after Olivia's first birthday, we'll start trying."

I didn't think my heart could be fuller, but hearing that... Well, I was wrong.

I kiss my wife. "I love you."

My mother's phone rings, and she quickly excuses herself. Rhett, Levi, Lily, Parker, and Uncle Jim gather in the living room to watch the babies and Parker open presents.

"Well, get to it." Uncle Jim coughs. "Let's see the little tank and angel tear open their first presents."

"We're just waiting on Mom," Lily says, glancing to the kitchen where Ma disappeared several minutes ago. "I don't know what's taking her so long."

"I got twenty that says Olivia gets her gift open first," Levi exclaims, slapping a twenty-dollar bill on the coffee table.

Rhett scoffs, pulling out his wallet. "You're on, bro. Have you seen Gage? The kid is going to rip his open in one fuckin' tear."

"Language!" Maci and Cassidy balk, earning a hearty laugh around the room.

My father grunts, tossing a twenty down as well. "I've got money on my little Livy."

Levi claps. "That's what I'm talkin' about. Anyone else?"

Uncle Jim thumbs through a wad of cash. "Gage."

Cassidy shakes her head. "I don't know... Gage has the strength, but Olivia is fast. She booty scoots quicker than Gage can throw toys."

Levi rubs his hands together. "Then this'll be a damn good wager."

Maci props Olivia up on her knee to burp her. "You guys can't bet on the babies like that."

"Shhh," I whisper. "Bean's got this. I've been training her on the sidelines."

Maci laughs.

I've never been happier than this moment. Who am I kidding? I've been saying that every day since I met her.

My mother slowly steps into the living room, her phone clutched to her chest with tears in her eyes. My father's sits up straighter. "What is it, Julie?"

"It's...Beau," she says. "He's coming home."

"About damn time," Uncle Jim says with a raise of his beer.

Mom starts to cry, and I share a concerned look with my siblings scattered around the room as my father stands to go to her. "H-He's been shot," my mother cries. "My baby's been shot."

The End.

Thanks for reading!
Please leave a review on Amazon or Goodreads to let me know what you thought!

Ready for more Montgomery brothers? Keep reading for a sneak peak of Beau's story in Book Three: Backed by You.

XO,
A. Boss

Backed by You

Beau

"I said, I don't need it," I growl, attempting to maneuver around the flight attendant holding out the cane they forced me onto this damn plane with.

"But Mr. Montgomery, you—"

I stalk past the woman and down the aisle to the exit. My knee is stiff from the long flight, but it's manageable. I've been doing physical therapy nonstop for the last four months—during and after sessions. After two knee surgeries to repair the tendons and muscle and a full joint replacement—that a single stray bullet destroyed—I'm walking.

And like hell I'll be seen using a damn cane at thirty-three.

Deboarding the plane, I toss my military-grade backpack over my shoulder and head to baggage claim. It's a surreal feeling being back in Montana. *Home.*

After serving my country for the last fifteen years, I've been honorably discharged from the Army. I wasn't ready to leave my brothers-in-arms behind, but life has a sick way of handing out cards, and this card...I'm going to have to play.

I'll be moving forward with my fallback plan of building and managing rental cabins in the popular ski resort mountains of Whitetail.

Between my parents and siblings, they've done a good job at managing my property and the two rentals while I've been away. But I'll be taking over everything. Hell, I'll need the distraction because after getting shot in the fucking knee, my military career is over.

My jaw ticks as I come around the corner at the congested airport in Whitetail. My entire family is lined up beside the baggage claim with 'Welcome Home Beau' signs.

Christ.

I mean, I get it. I haven't been home for over three years, but this isn't the homecoming I wanted. In fact, I didn't want one at all.

"There he is," my father booms.

"Beau," Ma shouts, rushing toward me.

I go through the motions of hugs and hellos. I plaster on a fake smile as best I can, but I'm willing to bet it looks more like a fucked-up grimace.

My four brothers, sister, my nephew, my parents—everyone looks about the same as when I saw them last. Except now, there are two women I don't recognize with babies on their hips and wedding rings on their fingers—my apparent 'sister-in-laws' Ma mentioned on the phone a few months ago.

Duke introduces me to his wife, Maci, and their ten-month-old daughter, Olivia—who looks exactly like her mother, with deep red hair and green eyes. While Butch introduces me to his wife, Cassidy, and their nine-month-old son, Gage—a mini version of Butch with his mother's blue eyes.

Half my siblings seem to have started a family while I was away. Even my nephew Parker has sprouted like a weed from the last picture Lily sent me.

Meanwhile, I haven't felt the embrace of a woman in...a long time.

My chest tightens at the thought.

"How the hell are you, Beau?" Duke grins, giving me a burly hug.

I grunt.

"You look good, man," Rhett says. "How's the knee?"

"Fine," I say, reaching for my duffle on the rotating belt beside me.

Levi snatches the bag at the last second. "I've got it, man." He winks, hefting it over his shoulder. "No worries."

I grit my teeth. This is going to be more frustrating than I anticipated.

You could say I've gotten along with my siblings over the years. Mainly because I keep my mouth shut and watch the bullshit from the sidelines.

Not that our personalities match in the slightest from what I can remember. I'm a loner; they're all about family. I joined the military; they started businesses and stayed close to home. Hell, I'm the only one who's ever left the country.

"Is that all you have, sweetie?" Ma asks.

"Yeah."

"Well, let's hit it, kids." My father claps. "Your mother's got a roast waiting at home that's calling my name."

There's a collective bit of laughter amongst everyone. Except me. I was hoping to go straight to the cabin.

Duke slaps a hand on my shoulder. "You're riding with us, bro."

We head to his truck and I take the front seat, while Maci and Olivia sit in the back. I stare out the window, taking in everything that's changed since the last time I was here.

"So, how was Washington DC?" my brother asks, glancing between me and the road. "Ma said that's where they sent you after they got you back stateside."

"Best knee surgeon in the States is stationed there," I grumble.

He nods. "You, uh, feeling good? I mean, ya look fuckin' great. Like you haven't taken a break from the gym or whatever the hell they had you doin' for recovery."

I've never been one to sit idly by when there's work to be done. Whether that's leading my squadron or pushing my body to heal—it's all the same to me.

Maci clears her throat. "We talked to Callie and let her know that if she needs anything to give you a call. But, um, we don't have your new phone number to give her."

My brow furrows. "Who?"

"Callie Ryan," Duke says, like I'm supposed to know who that is. "She's your tenant. She moved into the one-bedroom cabin, been renting it for the last four months."

"Almost five," Maci corrects.

Right. She's the one staying in *my* cabin. The one my mother was supposed to make sure was vacant for me when I got home. But lines got missed, and it was already rented out before I made it known I wanted it vacant for myself. "Got it."

"Maci and I, we've sort of taken over all the scheduling for the other cabin," he tells me. "Maci set you up a sweet website and everything. It's been blowing up with bookings."

Maci leans forward from the back with a kind smile. "I made sure it was free for you this weekend, though. Well, the next three nights at least. It's kind of booked after that..."

I scowl. *Fuck.*

"Ma thinks you're going to want to stay at the house, but I figured we'd offer up our spare bedroom before she hounded you," Duke says.

"Thanks, but I'll figure something out."

Duke raises a brow. "You sure, Beau? I mean, Butch's got a spare room, too. Rhett and Levi got a pullout couch. Wherever you want. Lily's working on moving out of Ma's finally, so if you really want to stay there, I doubt it'd be a big deal."

I huff. The idea of staying with any of my family sounds more fucking miserable than sleeping in the deserts of Iraq with active gunfire.

I don't need this kind of back-and-forth right out the gate.

"Um, there are breaks between bookings," Maci says quietly. "Usually so Julie can clean between renters, but, um, if you're looking for somewhere to stay, I'm sure you can in between. If you don't mind moving around to get a little privacy."

I nod. *That*, I can deal with.

Changing the subject, I ask, "Did you take a look at that truck I sent you? Is it worth the money for what I'm planning on doing with it?"

Duke sighs, rubbing the back of his neck. "Yeah, it's a good truck. I let Steve at the dealership know you were flying in today. Said he'd hold it for you to have a look for yourself."

"Good."

"You're not gonna take a fuckin' break to save your life, are you?" my brother mutters.

Not if I have anything to say about it.

"Duke. I've been sitting on my ass for the last five months. Working through recovery, physical therapy, and dealing with getting discharged. I don't need a fuckin' break, all right? What I do need is for everyone to get off my ass when I just got back in town."

He shakes his head, turning down the driveway to my parents' place.

Three years since I've set foot in Montana, since I've been home... Three long, lonely years. And all I want is to be left alone.

Get ready for the grouchiest Montgomery looking for love in
Backed by You,
Book Three: Montgomery Brothers of Montana!
Sign up for my newsletter at abossauthor.com and receive the FREE,
insta-love story of Clayton & Julie, prequel novella to Montgomery
Brothers of Montana!

Note from the Author

Thank you for choosing to pick up this book and read it! It means so much to me that you chose to spend your time reading something that I wrote. If I could hug you through this page, I would.

I hope you loved this enough to come back for more, because I certainly intend to put more out in the world from the *Boss Babe Universe*!

Don't forget to sign-up for my newsletter <u>HERE</u> and receive your *FREE* copy of *Only by You*, the insta-love story of Clayton & Julie, prequel novella to Montgomery Brothers of Montana!

Are you a *Boss Babe*?

Join the *Boss Babe Universe* on Facebook, Twitter/X, and Instagram!

About the Author

A. Boss proudly proclaims to be a romance enthusiast who just loves love! She's a simple writer who only recently found her love of writing and storytelling. When she's not diligently spilling her heart and soul into a word document, you'll find her hanging out with her loving husband, two crazy kids, and two sleepy dachshunds.

You can follow her on all the social media platforms for updates, freebies, and sneak peeks at upcoming releases. Twitter/X, Facebook, Instagram – whatever your poison may be – drop by and say hello!

Everyone is welcome in the *Boss Babe Universe*!

Acknowledgements

A huge thank you to my critique ladies and beta readers – Sarah (for naming baby Olivia Grace), Leah (for loving the Montgomerys), Colleen (for competency porn, lol), Jill (for the continued support), and Sevannah (for all the edit catches) - I appreciate all of you!

"Choose to surround yourself with people who inspire you, support you, and help you to grow into your happiest, strongest, wisest self."

Thank you!